Ghosts of the Connecticut River

Ghosts of the Connecticut River

Loretta Vandivier Rea

Order this book online at www.trafford.com
or email orders@trafford.com

Most Trafford titles are also available at major online book retailers.

Printed in the United States of America.

ISBN:978-1-4269-7255-3 (sc)
ISBN: 978-1-4269-7256-0 (e)

Library of Congress Control Number: 2011909721

Trafford rev. 06/20/2011

 www.trafford.com

North America & international
toll-free: 1 888 232 4444 (USA & Canada)
phone: 250 383 6864 ✦ fax: 812 355 4082

To Paul,
You make life
an adventure, mystery
and a love story. You encourage
with patience, inspire me and share my interests.
Thank you for following me to the
cornfield and for listening
to my stories.
I love you

Table of Contents

SMALL HAND PRINTS

IT WAS A perfect Indian Summer day for a ride in our yellow convertible, my husband's pride and joy. We put our two young daughters in the back seat, lowered the black cloth top, then pulled away from our new Rocky Hill, Connecticut home. Our move from the Midwest had been exhausting but we were unpacked and ready to check out our new neighborhood. Shortly after turning onto Route 160 toward Glastonbury, we stopped at a roadside stand to check out their decorative corn stalk bundles, yellow and purple mum plants as well as the end of the summer produce.

"How about some fresh apple cider?" the elderly lady asked, as she set out a small tray of four 3.5 oz plastic sample cups, just the right size for small hands to grasp. Our children eagerly downed the cloudy, sweet apple juice. "Headed for the ferry landing?" the old lady asked. "We are new to the area and out exploring today;
What's this about a ferry?' I asked.

"Up ahead is the country's oldest continuously operating ferry. It started as a raft guided with poles in 1655. At one time a horse on a treadmill in the center of the craft supplied the power to propel the craft across the Connecticut River," she added.

"In the late 1800"s, it became a steam driven craft. My grandmother was a little girl and attended the demonstration followed by a big celebration. She was crossing the river standing on the open flatboat with three other children and their dog. Water splashed up making the floor slippery. She held on tight to the wooden railing while the rocking made her feet slide around.

A boring speech had just ended when suddenly, without warning the band started playing. The startled dog barked then leaped out of the girl's arms and into the river. The two sisters lost their balance and fell in. Their slightly older brother jumped in but was unsuccessful in saving them or himself. My grandmother stood alone and could only watch her friends and their dog thrashing under the water. Their screams for help were not heard over the band music and they were lost," said the old lady. "My Grandmother never got over it."

We paid the old lady for a summer squash and four candy apples, then headed for our car. "Do you believe that story?"
I asked my husband. "I don't know, but now I have to see that ferry, and besides it cuts eight miles one way off the trip to Glastonbury."

When we arrived at the landing we saw a line of cars, bicyclists and pedestrians waiting to ride the ferry across the river. My husband got out of the car and started a conversation with another man who was also waiting. Our girls had fallen asleep in their car seats, so I pulled up the car's black cloth top enough to shade their sweet faces from the strong autumn sun.

I got out of the car, stood next to it and stretched my legs. Two cars and a truck drove onto the ferry and crossed the river. On the trip back it carried two cars, six pedestrians, and a bicyclist. It looked like one more time across and it would be our turn. The three cars ahead of us loaded on the ferry and it pulled away from the landing.

I heard the man tell my husband that the ferry today is towed by a diesel powered towboat. I listened closely to hear if my husband would ask about the old lady's story. Just then a young man and woman walking their bikes stopped next to me. I turned and started to talk, all the time wondering how I could work the drowning story question into the conversation.

Suddenly the car holding our two sleeping daughters started to roll toward the river. I screamed and chased after it. The sound of pounding

feet running behind me filled my ears as I witnessed my strapped in, sleeping, daughters headed toward a water grave. Our car picked up speed, headed straight toward the water, then abruptly stopped at the river's edge.

We grabbed the girls, held them tight and kissed them as we scanned the ground for a clue as to what stopped the run away car just in time.

A young man pointed to the hood of our car. There were three sets of small children's hand prints indented in the car metal.

APRIL 8TH

ANNIVERSARY GUESTS

OLIVIA VANDYGRIFF WAS being groomed to be the wife of a politician or an executive, so her high profile, prominent Bostonian parents didn't accept their oldest daughter's Italian immigrant husband, While enrolled at an all girl boarding school in Connecticut she met and had fallen in love with the young, handsome shipbuilder. She first spotted him while she and her classmates took a weekend outing to the Connecticut River shore.

She melted at the sight of his tanned, sculpted shoulders, dark determined eyes and high goals. He was the contrast to her pampered, slim, ivory form and undecided direction. It was on a dare that she boldly introduced herself while he was sitting alone one day eating his lunch.

Ponzio had come from Italy, along with his father to work in the Essex Shipyard. The two shared living space with several other male family members in a small cape style house in Centerbrook, built by the shipyard owners to house the immigrant workers. The shipyard workers took pride in their craft, worked very hard and sent most of their pay back to Italy. The collective dream was to some day be to able to bring their mothers and sisters to live in The United States.

Saturday morning, April 8, 1910 Olivia and Ponzio were married in the Egyptian Revival style Baptist Church. A school friend of Olivia's and Ponzio's father attended the brief wedding ceremony. Olivia was not at all surprised when her family didn't show up. The light lemon colored dress with matching cape was a far cry from the heavily beaded ivory satin wedding gown with leg of mutton sleeves, her mother had saved and hoped that all her daughters would wear at their weddings.

The five little girls spent many childhood hours giggling and dreaming over their parent's wedding photograph album. Their wedding had been the social affair of the year that merged two prosperous families.

The morning of Olivia's and Ponzio's wedding, he waited, paced, and prayed that his Olivia hadn't change her mind about marrying him that day. While he waited he picked her some wild flowers which served as her bridal bouquet.

The following April 8th, 1911, their first wedding anniversary. Olivia had hoped the letter she sent to her parents, containing the good news that she was pregnant and making them grandparents in a few months would soften their hearts. She had even fantasized about them opening their arms and throwing an anniversary dinner that would pale the lavish dinner parties they routinely hosted.

Apparently they weren't ready to accept Olivia's choice in a husband. Olivia and Ponzio would celebrate their first wedding anniversary alone and in their own way.

Ponzio continued to charm Olivia with his toothy grin and quick wit. They decided to have a late dinner picnic at the Connecticut River's shore near where they first met. They went down Main Street pretending to be a prosperous pair who lived in one of the mansions.

They admired the Victorian, Gothic and Federal styles as they fantasized and laughed. Once they arrived at the river's edge they spread their checkered blanket. Olivia opened the lid of the picnic basket and began pulling food out. She wanted their anniversary to be special. She set two bayberry candles in little tin candle holders while Ponzio dipped river water for the wild flowers they picked together for the anniversary picnic.

As Ponzio buttered a chunk of bread, he said, "I heard a story from the other shipyard workers. They said that nearly a hundred years ago in 1814, on this same date, April 8, the town of Essex was attacked and twenty eight ships were burned by British."

At that moment both candle flames suddenly went out. "That was strange," said Olivia. "I didn't feel a breeze."

Ponzio once again lit the candles while he continued, "The value of the damage was equal to the cost of two hundred very large, two story homes."

Olivia held her belly as she felt her baby move for the first time Ponzio said, "136 British marines and sailors rowed boats from four British warships anchored in Long Island Sound, up the Connecticut River to the foot of Main Street. "That's right near here," said Olivia.

This time only one candle went out and they could see shadows moving around them. The second candle's flame went out leaving them in total darkness. The frightened young pair grabbed at things in the dark. One reached for their picnic food, flowers; the other took the basket, candles and ran. When they got into the light they had in their hands, an antique sword and pistol, a Brown Bess musket, and an antique British marine helmet.

THE BELLOWS FALLS ARTIST

ALBERT HELD THE parchment invitation and read it to himself, for the second time.

" Clifford Baxter respectfully
invites your attention
to view specimens of his
art executed by himself
on August 8, 1849 at the
Connecticut River's edge
at Bellows Falls, Vermont."

Once at the art exhibit, Albert expected to be pursued for painting lessons, for which payment he could barter. If the truth be known, there was nothing he would love more than to learn to sketch and paint. But, being the oldest of nine children, his share of household chores seemed to him, endless. There just wasn't time for him to seriously pursue his interest in art, making his natural talent unrecognized and therefore not encouraged. The area boys and men were expected to work in the paper mill or for the railroad. The arts were not considered to be productive.

Albert set the art show invitation on the table and headed out for a walk. He did his best thinking while kicking rocks and shuffling down the gravel road. The hot summer sun pounded, glistening his skin and making him unaware that the dust he kicked up had started sticking to his arms and face.

Beyond a patch of wild, orange tiger lilies, overgrown grass and weeds, at an isolated spot at the river's edge, Mr. Baxter sat at his easel and painted. Long careful strokes formed on canvas, the image of the bridge over the Connecticut River, just before the Great Falls. The themes of the Baxter paintings were always the Connecticut River. He would vary the seasons, the angles. add people and wildlife.

"Hello, Mr. Baxter! Mind if I watch?" said Albert, unsure at first if the artist was aware he was there.

He continued to paint, without looking up, explained the composition, style and the prospective of his art work. Mr. Baxter, Albert's mother's second cousin was the only professional artist that Albert had ever met. Their interesting conversation met with competition for Albert's attention as a small boat drifted past them.

Its amateur navigators were two very attractive, young ladies, giggling and adjusting their large, straw sun hats. They hadn't noticed how far they had drifted, and were unaware that they were heading directly toward the falls. Their launch struck a submerged snag, careened and flipped over.

Shrill screams cut through the heavy humid air. Full skirted, heavy dresses, tangled with long hair, thrashed in the cold river water. Albert and the old artist bolted for the shore, shedding clothes and dropping them as they ran.

Albert, the stronger swimmer of the two men, summoned every last ounce of his strength to help the two young women to shore. His eyes scanned the river and landscape searching for Mr. Baxter. All he saw was one straw sun hat hung up on a submerged log caught by it's long blue ribbon ties. He looked farther down the Connecticut River and he saw the other hat spinning and twirling in the water as it danced out of sight.

Clara, the older of the two sisters rescued that day, and Albert were married years later. Mr. Baxter's body was never found. Albert as husband and father, also became an accomplished and well known portrait artist. But, oddly his fastest selling paintings, those supporting his family, were scenes of the Connecticut River. No one ever actually saw Albert painting his river paintings.

Albert, himself had been stunned and frightened in the beginning when he arrived at his art studio and found the still wet but completed Connecticut River paintings waiting there for his signature.

BURIED GOLD

I ALWAYS THOUGHT OUR tree service advertisement should read, "tree trimming, removal, fertilization, and insect removal; FULL SERVICE," seemed too broad. Now that ad got a job to construct Bald Eagle nests, 80 feet up in the canopy of mature Cottonwood trees, overhanging the Connecticut River.

My two brothers and I drove to Northfield, Massachusetts where we took a boat to Kidd's Island. Our instructions were to construct Bald Eagle nests by hoisting natural materials up and assembling them in the trees.

I had drawn the short straw, so Calvin supported the ladder and secured my safety straps. Harley twisted green saplings around twigs before he passed them up to me. Once the foundation for the nest was anchored I lined it with fallen leaves and soft grasses. As much as I had jokingly complained, this job was an interesting diversion from our everyday, routine tree service.

By the time we finished the third nest our conversation turned to summer camp and the Captain Kidd pirate story we enjoyed as young boys around the campfire.

According to the popular legend, Captain Kidd and his men ascended the Connecticut River searching for a distinctive but secluded place to bury their treasure chest of gold. What is now called Kidd's Island, had became their chosen place. As the legend goes, one man was killed and his body buried on top of the bounty to protect it from treasurer hunters.

It was William Kidd's misfortune to sail as the rules changed and acts of piracy became outlawed. The line drawn between officially sanctioned acts and piracy was a thin one. You were legitimate when Queen Elizabeth I sanctioned your voyage, and then took home a share of the loot.

Corruption and greed ran rampant as actions condoned by one group were considered illegal by another. Caption Kidd had been commissioned to protect the English colonies against attacks.

The royal navy squadron became convinced that Kidd was up to no good. He became desperate after he developed scurvy and his ship started leaking. He felt all legal options were gone so he and his men attacked, gaining gold, silk, muslin, calico, and sugar.

The word had been sent out from England that Kidd should be considered a pirate. Kidd sold the bulky cargo for gold, burned his distinctive, sinking ship and he and his men made their way to Block Island carrying the hope of a pardon, with the help of his rich and powerful New York friends.. It is said that in the summer of 1699 they somehow made their way up the Connecticut River and buried the gold on Kidd's Island. Soon after, Kidd was captured and thrown in jail in Boston, then shipped to England where he stood a one day trial. During the first attempt of execution, the rope broke. A second rope was put around his neck and he was successfully hanged for murder and multiple piracies.

"Wow," I said, "I haven't thought about that tale since I was a kid".

Harley leaned on the shovel and joked, "We're here, there is a full moon, there are three of us. What have we got to lose? A full moon directly overhead lighted a spot on the ground. Could this be Kidd's buried treasure spot? One minute after midnight, the three men formed a triangle and worked in silence. Any words or noise could break the charm. They took turns shoveling deeper and deeper as sweat ran down their backs, down their foreheads, and into their eyes.

One by one, the three silently tossed their shirts. A force of mosquitoes swarmed, then bore down, biting, but the men ignored the discomfort. What started out as a light hearted curiosity had now slowly developed into a serious mission. Not one of the three grown men could have anticipated earlier in the day that before sunrise they would be frantically digging for buried pirate's gold. The metal shovel hit something. Was that a skull or a rock?

The brothers looked at each other, speechless and remembering not to make a sound. They studied each other's eyes in the faint full moonlight.

Suddenly the moon was blocked by the eighty-five inch wing span each of two adult Bald Eagles. Their eyes glared like little balls of fire as they dived, free falling, then pulled in their strong, sharp, claws and ATTACKED!.

THE PIECES FIT

THE RED HOT melted copper flowed into the sand mold and settled into shape. Paul wiped the perspiration from his forehead, catching it just before it burned his eyes. Last night he had worked late to finish an order of tools for the sawmill. He had worked at the foundry long enough to be comfortable to occasionally create small works of art from scrap, on his own time. This morning he arrived early and fired up, eager to make a design he thought of during the night. He twisted two thin hot copper strands to fit together to form a ring. The outside twist fit his finger and he hoped the smaller, inside twist would fit Sarah's finger.

The young couple often secretly met at Havenhill dock. Sarah was the sweetest and the most beautiful girl that Paul had ever seen. He picked up the picnic basket with one hand and helped her into the boat with the other arm. The couple rowed to the center of the Connecticut River.

Once their small boat was positioned, they floated and drifted in the cold, deep, unobstructed flow to Bugbee Landing. As the boat docked, Five wading Sandpipers took flight toward the white laden sky.

The two had fallen in love but Sarah's parents objected to their nine years age difference.

"What is this?" Sarah asked when Paul dropped the intertwined copper strands into her hand. The two wavy circles fell apart in her palm. "The ring is actually two rings," Sarah noticed. She studied the two circles then shyly smiled at Paul.

"Try on the small ring," Paul said. But, he couldn't wait so he picked it up and slid it onto her finger. It was a perfect fit.

"What does this ring mean? asked Sarah.

"To me it means you are my better half and some day we won't have to hide our feelings for each other," answered Paul.

The next day Paul thought of Sarah as he put in his time at the foundry. The heat was like that of a furnace but in his mind he was drifting on the cool water looking into Sarah's sweet young face.

"Stay away from my little girl," shouted Sarah's angry father. He shoved the small copper ring in Paul's hand and left the foundry as suddenly as he arrived,

The next time Paul saw Sarah's father would be later that same week, under tragic circumstances. There had been an accident while Sarah watched her younger siblings at the river's edge. One minute she laughed and kicked water, the next she slipped and cracked her head on a wet pile of rocks.

From the doorway, Paul saw beautiful Sarah, in her coffin surrounded by mounds of white, red, yellow and pink flowers. The entire community was shocked. She wore a wreath of fresh flowers on her head, a sheer, delicate white dress and held her white Bible in her hands.

Sobbing friends and neighbors surrounded the grieving family.

Paul slipped up to the coffin unnoticed. Sarah looked even younger and more innocent to him now. Her right hand lie on top of her left hand, pressing the white Bible against her flat abdomen. Paul pulled Sarah's ring from his pocket and slid it onto the ring finger of her cold, rigid, lifeless left hand. He placed her right hand back on top and her ring could not be seen.

If Sarah's family and friends saw Paul sitting at the back during the funeral, no one acknowledged his presence. At the cemetery he watched from behind a heavily wooded spot as her coffin was lowered into the earth, then piled high with flowers.

Many years passed and the broken hearted Paul vowed never to marry. He remained loyal to the memory of his lovely Sarah and never even looked at another woman. Then, during the middle years of his life, he became friends with a charming widowed lady. She had been left to raise three young sons by herself. Paul convinced himself that what they had was no more than a friendship and he took an interest in guiding the fatherless boys into young manhood.

Eventually even he had to admit to himself that he had fallen in love, not only with Laura, but also her three boys. He wished for a sign of approval from Sarah but nothing happened. He dismissed the thought to ever act on his feelings.

Later that summer Paul, Laura and her sons floated down the Connecticut River to fish. "Let's stop at Havenhill Dock," said Ethan, Laura's youngest son. As they pulled the boat to shore the sandpipers fought over something shinny on the glistening wet sand. There on the sand was Sarah's half of their copper wire ring. Paul took his half off his finger and twisted in her half before setting it on a rock. As he looked at it, thinking, trying to take it all in, a white dove flew in from nowhere, picked up the entwined rings and flew away with it in her beak.

THE CRAMPED LEG

B RENDON MCINTYRE RUBBED his aching legs. It was the end of another day of logging on the Connecticut River. He was part of the group of boys who liked to squeeze in a game of log birling when ever they could. One boy would start "walking the log", causing it to roll in the water while his competitor, on the other end of the log tried to keep his balance and avoid a splash into the frigid Connecticut River water. The lumberjacks objected to the horseplay, especially during serious log drives, but they couldn't work and watch everyone at the same time, plus the local boys were cheap laborers.

Brendon's parents, Colleen McKenna and Dunchad McIntyre had moved to Gill, Massachusetts from Ireland in 1885, Ignoring the pleas of their large, tight knit families left back in Ireland, they arrived separately and waited to be married privately in America. Brendon, the first of eight children, was born just before their second wedding anniversary

Colleen sold pillows that she sewed at home, while raising the large, young family. Dunchad worked full time at the saw mill and part time at the grist mill. To make ends meet, the family also raised corn and rye which they sent to Boston and sold. Over the years Brendon held various odd jobs. He and his wife opened a saloon. Usually business was slow except when the hundreds of tough river men descended on Turner Falls from the river's headwaters near Quebec. The north wood's streams and brooks flushed out 40-foot-long spruce logs when the snow melted.

In the spring, 250,000 logs traveled 300 miles, reached stretches of the Connecticut River white-water rapids, then many jammed. Brendon began getting up in years, but he still worked freeing the logs. Sometimes he dove into the river to physically free the logs and other times he used dynamite.

One day in April, while freeing logs, Brendon treaded the icy Connecticut River water until he was near exhaustion. He pulled and pushed, unable to untangle a small, twine like pine branch before it began to hog tie his feet at the ankles. He was being pulled under as he spotted a huge log barreling toward him, aiming at his head. The log dipped in a swirling water whirlpool, slammed into Brandon, crushing his right leg against the Lower Suspension Bridge's stone pier foundation.

Four northern lumberjacks pulled him from the river. His mangled right leg dangled, barely still connected to his body. A twisted red and black plaid flannel shirt, served as a tourniquet.

His body was icy cold from the water and Brandon was given whiskey for the pain. A single sweep of a razor sharp logging knife through the flesh, followed by a swift stroke of the lumberjack's hatchet through the bone and the useless leg was off.

One of the men dug a hole along the river bank and tossed in the bloody, mangled leg, still wearing the wool sock and spiked logging boot. As time passed Brandon's stump healed over and he walked wearing a wooden peg prosthesis.

Mysteriously, although his stump healed and was no longer tender to the touch, he felt a phantom cramping in the area of the missing calf, ankle and toes.

For days he searched for the unmarked spot along the river bank that had become his mangled leg's grave. He didn't know the name of the lumberjack who buried his leg and had long ago migrated to another area.

Brandon was certain he could get some relief if only the severed limb could be located, dug up, repositioned and properly reburied.

He suffered in agony with the phantom leg cramping. He was at home with his wife in 1936 when the gushing great flood brought hundreds of logs ramming through the riverbed, plowing up soil and ripping up small trees.

Suddenly his phantom leg pain was gone. He stood up and walked around, enjoying the absence of pain for the first time since his awful accident.

Down near the river, the town's people scurried for safe high ground by way of Route 2 and Miller's Falls Road just as the old suspension bridge was washed away. Frank Miller, a childhood friend of Brandon's saw something floating in the flood debris. He retrieved the waterlogged leg and boot. Before he could reach Brandon to tell him that he found his leg Brandon died of a heart attack.

Two days later, Brandon and his leg were reunited in the grave.

PREMATURE DEATH

FIFTEEN WHITE CALLA Lilies, pointing in the same direction, were backed by waxy lemon leaves, and secured with a black ribbon bow. The fresh flower wreath on the front door signified the death in the family of Archibald Sullivan of Colebrook, New Hampshire.

The sun rose, birds sang, life went on, and the milk-man delivered milk. "Read all about it", the newspaper boy chanted..

Didn't they know I died? I pushed a newspaper off the rack. I bet they thought it was the wind. It actually was a breeze that blew open the paper to the obituaries.

"Jeremiah T. Sullivan, August 8, 1888 – July 25, 1903. It is with regret we record the death of our young fellow citizen. The funeral took place on Sunday morning. The remains had lain in the deceased's family home. An immense concourse of citizens of all classes sent condolences of flowers, food and telegrams to the sorrowing family in this, their sad hour of bereavement for the premature demise of their gifted lad. Prayers at the grave were recited by Rev. Father Brophy. Jeremiah T. Sullivan, son of Catherine and Archibald Sullivan, succumbed when he was seized with an epileptic fit in the Connecticut River."

There it was in black and white. I had died. I died being deprived of perpetuating the species, nurturing a family and achieving my potential. I died deprived of the fun of my beloved practical jokes and pranks. I'm dead yet justifiability annoyed.

The town cabinetmaker, also the town embalmer (convenient source for coffins), embalmed me in the family bathtub at home.

My mother dressed me while Aunt Sarah hung dark colored drapes to transform our parlor into a funeral parlor.

I saw my grandparents holding each other and sobbing. People I barely knew and I didn't think cared about me, came by the house bringing food and flowers. My parents sat silently staring. I wished I could take away their pain.

I had an idea to make my sisters smile. I took the form of a Monarch butterfly and landed on Isabella's shoulder.

"Don't move," instructed Rachel. She offered her finger and I, in the form of a butterfly, stepped on. She ever so carefully brought her hand with my orange butterfly wings resting on her finger, around to Isabella's face.

"Shhh, don't scare it." warned Rachel. The two girls sat in the clover talking to me as the butterfly as I went from one to the other before flying away.

My brother, Noah sat sobbing in the tool shed. We used to entertain ourselves by playing practical jokes on each other. I tapped on the door.

"Who is it?" he called out. Again, tap, tap, tap; this time he rose and walked toward the door.

I slipped the nail through the latch so he couldn't open the door. "Jeremiah, is that you?" he asked , looking toward the little shed's ceiling. He didn't know that I was standing right behind him. You should have seen his jaw drop after I unlocked the shed door and let it freely swing open.

My mother went about her household chores like a mindless, emotionless, puppet. She didn't smile or even speak much. She carried a stack of just washed, line dried, cotton bed sheets upstairs. She bent over the bed and shook the sheet into the air. It floated to the bed and she quickly tucked in the corners. She repeated the task, this time with the top sheet. Tears fulled her eyes as she jammed the down pillow into the pillowcase. She had embroidered it for her hope chest, when she was a young girl. She had never considered her life would include one day burying a fifteen year old son. She finished the bed by topping it with the quilt Grandma had made for them for their wedding gift.

After she left the bedroom I pulled back the quilt, tossed the pillow onto the rocking chair in the corner, loosened all the sheet corners and rolled the sheets into a ball in the center of the bed.

Mother glanced into the bedroom on her way downstairs.

"Rachel, Isabella, Noah!" she shouted, then remembered she was alone in the house. She climbed back up the stairs, entered the bedroom and the bed was again neatly made. Neatly made to a fifteen year old boy ghost's standards.

You dare to question if this story is really true? Let me tell you that these Remington typewriter keys are pressing down, striking against the paper, the black and red spool ribbon and the cylinder roller, without anyone insight. The carriage return slides "by it's self?" to the next line. Who is doing it? Who is writing this?

The next time you get locked out of our house, misplace your library card, lose your homework, call a tow truck then the car starts before it arrives, it might be me! Or it could be a friend or relative who has passed.

THE GHOST BRIDE'S WARNING

D EBRA COULD HARDLY keep her thoughts on work. She went through the motions of preparing to be away from her job at the bank to go on her Niagara Falls, honeymoon for two weeks. Her mind kept going back to the many details of her soon to arrive wedding day.

She had met Robert when he came through her teller line at the bank. He was new to Portland and opened an account with his first paycheck from the golf shop he managed. Every Friday he would tease and make jokes as he deposited his pay at her teller window. One day he finally got the courage to ask her to go for a ride in his new 1953, red Buick Skylark. They had been together since that afternoon, two years ago.

"Debbi, you need to try on your wedding gown for Mrs. Martin, her mother reminded. Mrs. Martin was an elderly neighbor with talent for sewing.

Over the years Mrs. Martin created masterpieces of satin and lace with pearls. Nothing pleased the old woman more than to see the peaches and cream glow dotted with sparkling sapphire eyes, of a beautiful young bride-to-be trying on the wedding gown. A gown she had designed and sewn just for her.

Mrs. Martin sat on a low stool, holding pins pinched between her lips, until she needed them. Debra stood straight and tall as she slowly turned. The full skirted gown of the 50's with a crinoline showed off her tiny waist and long legs. Mrs. Martin carefully pinned layers of silk tulle over the skirt.

"There, look at yourself in the mirror, dear," Mrs. Martin said.

Debra gazed over her shoulder, admiring her own striking silhouette. She paused, and when she fully turned, she saw a grey, stern face wearing a bridal veil directly behind her. Debra blinked and the image disappeared. She became weak in the knees and Mrs. Martin saw that the blood had left her face.

"What's the matter, child?" asked the old woman. "You look like a ghost, or as though you just saw one".

"I think I'm just overly tired tonight, can we finish this another time?" asked Debra.

By the next morning, Debra had convinced herself that the ghost bride she saw in the mirror must have been her imagination and actually only shadows from the huge maple tree just outside the window.

"Finished!" announced Mrs. Martin, raising both arms as though she were a runner, crossing the finish line of a race. Debra beamed then nearly tripped as she stepped down and rushed toward the full length mirror.

"No, wait! This is a special moment, let's call your mother in to see you," Mrs. Martin proudly suggested.

Once again, standing directly behind Debra in the mirror was the grey, stern faced ghost bride. Her hair was pulled up leaving ringlet wisps of hair around her tiny face. She was beautiful but looked very serious almost to the point of being angry. Her grey wedding dress hung without much shape and she carried a huge arm bouquet of calla lilies, ivory roses, fern and forget-me-nots.

Debra's jaw dropped, her eyes filled with tears and she held her right hand to her heart, unable to speak, gasping for air.

"You do look breathtakingly beautiful, Debbi, baby" said her mother with tear filled eyes.

"No, oh no! I saw a ghost bride in the mirror! Didn't either of you see her?"

Mrs. Martin quickly said, "I bet that is Sophia, I've seen her before myself. She won't hurt you, she just longs to be near weddings. She stands in the background to watch the preparations for the festivities, then, quietly and quickly exits."

Mrs. Martin went on to tell, "In the late 1800's she was a young woman, the oldest of six daughters in the family. Many young, local men tried to get her attention. But, Seth, Sophia's friend since childhood was especially persistent and very determined that she would one day be his wife. Seth asked Sophia's father for a job at his restaurant where the entire family worked. He would do anything to be near Sophia every day.

Seth watched with disbelief as he started to suspect that beautiful Sophia was falling in love with the strong, blond, Polish immigrant that Sophia's father had hired to wash dishes.

Soon, it was no longer a secret that Sophia Santro and Rafal Stanslaw were in love, engaged and planning their wedding. Sophia's five younger sisters kept talk of the wedding plans going constantly as they cooked, seated guests, bussed tables, worked the register and cleaned at their family's restaurant. Seth tried to tell Sophia that he had always loved her, but she thought he was teasing and she laughed at him.

One week before Sophia's and Rafal's wedding the dress was finished and hanging in Sophia's closet. The flowers had been carefully selected and ordered for both the ceremony, as well as for tables at the restaurant reception. The menu was finalized and food had been ordered, prepared and stored.

Sophia, her mother and sisters finished at the restaurant and went home. "Remember to lock up when you're finished," Sophia's dad had reminded them earlier before he left.

Sophia had just arrived home when she received a telephone call to return to the restaurant. "Now what?" she asked herself, as she left the house. "I'll be back in a few minutes," she said.

The next morning, Sophia didn't present herself at the breakfast table; nor had she slept in her bed. The family rushed to the restaurant but no one was there. Had Sophia and Rafal eloped?

Sophia's handbag and restaurant keys were beside the locked, cash register drawer,

Promptly at 7 o'clock a.m. Rafal arrived ready to work. On this morning the entire family was frantically searching for their beloved Sophia. Seth was still here when I left the restaurant last night." said Rafal.

No one saw Seth on that day, and he didn't show up for work, the next day, or even the next. Had Seth and Sophia run away together? The question was wondered but never spoken. The entire Portland community searched for the beautiful, bride-to-be, Sophia. Each day dragged on painfully and Rafal felt sick with worry.

Sunday, June 22, 1902 The Portland Reporter landed on the hall table nearly knocking off the framed wedding invitation. Next to "We .request your presence at the marriage of our daughter, Sophia to Rafal Stanslaw, Sunday, June 22, 1902, at 2 O'clock," lay the newspaper headline, "Body Of Missing Young Woman Found In The Connecticut River."

When Seth was finally found, he confessed to strangling Sophia during his unsuccessful, jealous plea, for her to call off the wedding to Rafal and to marry him instead.

Rafal was unable to recover from his broken heart and never married.

Debra's last day to work at the bank before her wedding turned out to be a day of well wishes from the small town's bank's many patrons. At noon, Debra's co-workers had a cake and gifts for her in the lunchroom. After the little party, she went to the ladies room to freshen up before taking her place back at her teller's window.

While alone in the ladies room, Debra leaned close into the mirror. Suddenly she was startled speechless. The beautiful face of Sophia was behind her. She turned but no one was there.

Then a sweet young voice warned, "Get out of here! Get out of this bank building immediately! You are in danger!"

Debra quickly gathered her gifts, cards, handbag, keys and left through the back door. She drove straight home and when she arrived, a special report broke into the regular scheduled television programming to announce a bank robbery and hostage situation at the bank where she worked and had left just in time, unharmed.

ELIZABETH

I WAS SIX MONTHS pregnant with our first child in 1950. Keith and I were thrilled but also aware that a new family member, would change our lives forever.

"Let's get away for a long weekend," Keith suggested.

I packed our bags and we left from our home in Middletown, Connecticut and drove toward Grafton County, New Hampshire. Autumn was and still is ,my favorite season of the year. The sight of the Sugar Maples from atop Sunset Hill Ridge are breath taking; I remembered them from my visits as a child.

My Aunt Bea and Uncle Hilbert would take us up to the ridge for the panoramic views of both the White Mountains and the Green Mountains. Then, Uncle Hilbert and Daddy would play 9 holes at the Sugar Hill House Golf Course while Aunt Bea, Mother, and my sister, Susan and I would go over to McIndoe Falls on the Vermont side of the Connecticut River.

"It will be wonderful to visit Aunt Bea and Uncle Hilbert again. It's been too long," I told Keith

We drove north through Connecticut and on up through Massachusetts. The afternoon turned to evening, then late night. We both became exhausted and decided to stay the night at a little bed and breakfast just across the state line into New Hampshire.

A lady named Molly answered the door and told us how lucky we were that she had a vacant room during peak leaf season. I remember the wallpapered bedroom and pulling back the beautiful quilt on the bed but nothing after that. The next morning while Keith was in the shower, I turned to notice the bed was already made. Keith never did that before and how did he do it? He was in the shower. We dressed, put our bags in the car and went to the dinning room for breakfast.

"I have a strange feeling about this place," I whispered to Keith. I looked down and my silverware had moved across the table next to Keith's.

Molly poured coffee into my cup as she asked, "How is everything?"

I looked at Keith, waiting for him to speak. He gave me a look and I knew what he was thinking. You're pregnant, you're tired and your hormones are giving you an overactive imagination.

Turning to Molly, I said, "Some strange things have happened. I have an uneasy feeling."

"So, you've experienced our ghost!' Molly pulled out a chair from the next table and sat with us. In a half whisper and twinkling eyes, she said, "Elizabeth was in her early twenties when she married a much older English Sea Captain. The captain had been away at sea for more than a year and returned to Nashua, New Hampshire to find his wife had just given birth. He knew the baby could not have been his and he flew into an uncontrollable rage. He killed the newborn baby girl and buried her.

The captain nearly went out of his mind with anger and locked Elizabeth in a closet to punish her. Elizabeth escaped the closet, discovered her baby daughter gone and confronted the captain. During the argument they struggled, he stabbed her to death and threw her in a well.

We often sense the presence of Elizabeth. Guests report seeing her in the ladies room and peering through windows. She appears more often to women and loves to play with children.

She has been known to roll a ball back and forth on the floor with them. She turns lights on and off and more than once has thrown dishes through the air, smashing them against the wall.

Several guests at different times have reported hearing a baby's cry when there was none here. We called in a psychic from Gloucester, Massachusetts and a séance was performed. Elizabeth appeared that night with long flowing white hair and wearing a floor length, sheer white gown with light blue ribbons. She must have either returned or never left." said Molly.

I couldn't finish my breakfast. Keith paid the bill and I hurried to the car. I waited, wanting to get as far away as possible FAST! Keith bought a newspaper and chatted with the newsboy.

Later, in the car Keith asked, "You don't really believe that story, do you? Stories like that create interest for the tourists."

I turned my head and looked out my window. I didn't want to argue with my husband and I wasn't going to let "Elizabeth" ruin this weekend.

Early in the afternoon we arrived at Lisbon. The place hadn't changed much. I seemed smaller than when I was a kid.
Aunt Bea and Uncle Hilbert welcomed us with hugs.

I had decided to forget about the ghost story and I did not mention it to anyone. Maybe Keith was right about my being tired, my hormones and ghost stories entertain the tourists; I hoped so.

We rented a boat at East Ryegate and drifted down the Connecticut River.

"Have you kids chosen a name for your baby?" asked Aunt Bea.

"Robert if it's a boy, "I said, "we haven't decided for a girl ."

Aunt Bea said, "I've always loved the name "Elizabeth."

Behind her stood a beautiful, smiling, young ghost with long white hair and a flowing white dress with light blue ribbon.

THE CLOWN GHOST

I T WAS MUGGY and the sun
hovered that day in July, 1944
in Hartford, Connecticut. Sandra Sue Wilson had taken the day off from
slaving away at her job at the war production plant. World War II was
grinding on and she felt guilty about all the time spent away from her
family, due to the plant's mandatory overtime.

This year she decided to throw a special party to celebrate her
daughter, Rosemary's 8th birthday. The surprise party for Rosie would
have a circus theme.

A month earlier Grandma and Grandpa Wilson had taken Rosemary
and her sister, Maryann to the circus when it was in New Haven. In
the weeks since, the circus traveled to Bridgeport, Connecticut then
to Massachusetts, New Hampshire, Maine, and Rhode Island before it
returned to Connecticut. The circus had been all that the two girls had
talked about since. Rosemary and Maryann played for hours, drawing
pictures of high flying performers, clowns and circus animals.

When they tired of playing "circus" with their dolls, poor old Rex, the
overweight family dog, endured grueling training sessions to jump through

a hoop while wearing a ruffle collar. Mr. Yates, the mailman often stopped for a few minutes and watched them play circus.

Today the circus train arrived in Hartford. The girls had begged to see the circus again, but settled for an early morning outing to the north end to watch them set up the tent. The lions ate, the elephants took a hose bath while the acrobats rehearsed. It was the next best thing to actually attending the show again.

The tent had been waterproofed with a mixture of gasoline and paraffin. The circus had tried to get a hold of a new canvas flame proofing compound developed by the Armed Services but the Army could not release it for civilian use.

While the girls were away, watching the circus setting up, Sandra decorated the house for the surprise party. Mr. Yates, delivered the mail, and offered to come back to the party dressed as a clown after he finished his mail route. Sandra was delighted. A clown at the circus birthday would be the perfect, unforgettable touch.

Eight little girls, wearing paper hats, sat squirming with anticipation. The front door opened as Maryann and Rosemary walked into the decorated living room.

"Surprise!" was shouted, then , , , , , , , ,

"Happy birthday to you, happy birthday to you, happy birthday dear Rosie, happy birthday to you." the entire giggling group sang off key. Sandra carried in a yellow cake with chocolate icing, eight pink candles and a circle of circus animal crackers.

The door bell rang, Sandra waded through the small crowded living room, as she stepped over fallen pink and yellow crape paper streamers. She picked up off the floor, a pretty wrapped gift and set it on the table on her way to answer the door.

Mr. Yates was a little late but there stood the smiling clown. The girls squealed with delight. Sandra was surprised at how authentic Mr. Yates looked. He walked in and started twisting balloon animals for everyone, then entertained with a few magic tricks. Something didn't seem right, but the girls were enjoying the party and Sandra was tired and too distracted to give it much thought. The girls thoroughly enjoyed watching the clown who didn't speak, perform Sandra had no idea that Mr. Yates was a talented clown.

Ambulance and fire truck sirens could be heard in the distance, coming from the north. The telephone rang at the same time that mothers frantically appeared at the front door.

"Hello?" Sandra picked up the phone during the confusion.

"Mrs. Wilson, this is Wilbur Yates. I'm sorry I couldn't make it to your party. There is an emergency; a terrible fire over here at the circus. The bandleader was the first to notice the flames. A high wire act was performing when the fire broke out on a side wall of the enormous Big Top. In minutes flaming drops of liquid fire showered a panicked audience. Thousands of people, mostly children stampeded trying to escape. They crawled under and over the steel railings along the front of the bleachers. An animal chute blocked the main exit. People slashed holes in the tent's sides with pocketknives. It looks like hundreds of people have been injured, trampled and burned to death. I can't talk; others need to use the phone." Then the phone went dead.

Sandra turned to see mothers holding their daughters and crying. Everyone was in shock.

Sandra asked "If that was Wilbur just now on the phone, Then, who is the clown? Where is the clown?" One of the mothers just pointed, unable to speak. Rosemary looked pale and scared as she whispered, "Mommy, he vanished by walking right through that wall."

PATCHES

HE WORE HIS entire wardrobe all at once, even during the hottest of days during New England summers. His hair was matted and moved as a unit when he turned his head. The rest of his belongings stayed within his sight in the rusted wire grocery cart he pushed. Mismatched gloves covered his hands even though the fingers had worn off. He was likeable and known by everyone along the small Connecticut River town.

He never asked for anything, in fact, no one ever heard him speak.

The community looked after him and called him, "Patches". When the church had their ham and bean supper, a plate was taken to Patches. The same was true when the Lion's Club had their fish fry and the Boy Scouts sold pork chop meals.

Patches collected the empty soft drink cans tossed by people not interested in recouping their five cent deposit. Patches was accepted liked and had been somewhat of a mascot or a small town celebrity. People left food for him and even occasionally "Patches" would be mentioned in the weekly neighborhood newspaper.

My mother asked about him when she and Daddy first moved to Windsor, Connecticut. She was told that Patches had been a handsome, sensitive, serious, businessman, madly in-love with his fiancée'. She had been his entire world; he had lived for her. Veronica had long, natural curly, flame red hair, a slender build and flirtatious personality. She was full of life and passion, and together they made a striking young couple. Occasionally they would argue over Veronica's flirting with other men. There had been rumors that she regularly cheated on him but he either hadn't heard them, turned a blind eye or was in denial.

The day arrived for the anticipated wedding. Everyone in town was there and it had the promise of being "THE WEDDING" of the year. The groom, beamed with joy, as he stood waiting with his best man and groomsmen at the alter. One by one, lovely bridesmaids wearing rose pink, waltz length dresses, and carrying large arm bouquets walked down the aisle. The music played an additional song TWICE, guests began looking at one another, whispering, then turned and looked toward the back of the church, searching for answers to the delay. The maid of honor appeared in a floor length, pale pink gown. Her face was flushed; her eyes red and swollen as she hurried down the aisle, ignored the beat of the music then handed a note to the groom.

Veronica had changed her mind and she eloped with someone else that morning. The groom never got over being left at the alter by his beloved Veronica. Some say he lost his mind that day and slowly began turning into the person the community affectionately nicknamed, "Patches/"

One day, years later, Patches was found dead of natural causes, at his favorite spot by the river. The Community went together and buried him in style.

I had heard of the fancy grave monument and that it was something to see. I called my friend Kelly, who promised that she would meet me there, then canceled when she had to work late. I went alone, wandering through a poison-ivy strewn graveyard. There it was, a four foot tall marble stone monument with a bronze plaque which read, "Patches, a man often misunderstood but always deeply loved, 1863 – 1954."

I stood back and examined the stone for a moment. No expense spared here, I thought. A lot of people loved that strange, mysterious, misunderstood man. I wish I had known him, I think that I would have liked him. I felt a strange connection to this man I had never met.

Later, at home the evening proceeded normally. I read my mail, paid a couple of bills, then fed Tar Baby, my four legged, lap loving companion. He is a Bombay feline with a sable coat, like black leather.

Tar Baby could communicate with me through his beautiful copper penny eyes. Tar Baby and I had co-habituated since he was twelve weeks old. Alike in many ways, that cat and I shared the same easy going temperament and robust nature.

I flipped through the television channels and settled on a game show. During a commercial break in the show I looked through the cupboard for something to eat.

"Why didn't I go to the grocery store this afternoon?" I asked Tar Baby. He slinked around my feet in a figure eight pattern, letting his tail twist around my legs. He did that when he was happy with a full tummy.

I made myself a peanut butter, mayonnaise and lettuce sandwich then stood over the sink eating it. I heard the squeak the front door makes when it opens. I was sure I had closed it firmly then locked it, a good habit I developed over my years of living alone. Tar Baby acted strangely. He arched his back while taking a few steps sideways.

"what's the matter Scaredy Cat, see a ghost?" I asked.

The channel on the television had changed. In the living room, I also noticed the table lamp had been turned on.

I walked in a daze to the kitchen, intending to wash my knife and put away the peanut butter and mayonnaise. I must have forgotten that I did it, because that was already done. Odd things happened. I told myself I was being over imaginative and silly.

The next night, while watching television with Tar Baby sitting on my lap, I pulled back my crimson colored, curly hair and secured it with a hair clip. I felt a presence in the room, but it didn't frighten me. Tar Baby glanced me a look that read "I tried to tell you."

When I mentioned to Kelly that I thought I was living with a ghost; she laughed. That's the best excuse I've heard yet for natural aging forgetfulness," she had teased.

That was until she stopped in one Saturday morning for coffee and witnessed Tar Baby rolling his ball back and forth across the floor with someone that she and I couldn't see. Then the morning newspaper pages turned by themselves.

"He keeps the dishes washed, rearranges the furniture to suit himself and turns off lights. I call him "Patches".

FRIENDLY INDIAN

T HIS VACATION WAS going to be different than any before. Ken and I had raised four sons and a daughter in our New York City apartment. The youngest, in college and the others grown and raising their own children. Over the years our family vacations centered around the kids and their interests. We took in amusement parks from Florida to Ohio, visited relatives, went camping, visited Amish country and visited colleges.

There we were with an empty nest and still full of energy. Ken suggested a bicycle trip with a bicycle club, kayaking or mountain hiking.

"Hon, we're sixty-eight years old," I reminded him.

The fear of spending fourteen days sitting on a tiny, hard, triangular bicycle seat, while wearing a helmet, or pulling on hiking boots, prompted me to offer alternative suggestions.

"Let's drive upstate to Niagara Falls. We haven't been there since our honeymoon." He agreed, and we set out. The first mile was as beautiful and pleasant as the following three hundred, ninety-nine mile drive. It was a nice leisurely chance to stop and see sights along the way.

We got an early start, then stopped after a couple of hours and ate a big country breakfast at a little out of the way Mom and Pop spot. The restaurant was in Collinsville, Connecticut, next to the old ax factory.

Early afternoon we took in the Basketball Hall of Fame in Springfield, Massachusetts, then drove out route 90 for dinner and the night in Boston.

This was the best vacation ever. In the morning, without a plan, we headed northwest through Massachusetts into Vermont. We stopped for lunch at St Johnsbury, then drove eight miles south through farmland and forests along winding rivers and streams. To our delight, we stumbled across Barnet Village, part of a cluster of quaint villages on the Connecticut River. We wandered through Barnet Center, East Barnet, McIndoe Falls, Mosquitoville, Passumpsic then West Barnet.

Ken had tied the kayak to the top of the car and decided to look for Harveys Lake. I stayed back and toured specialty shop after shop. What a great afternoon of shopping. I bought Vermont Maple syrup in little glass maple leaf shaped bottles, cheddar cheese, apple-maple chutney, Vermont Teddy Bears for the youngest grand kids and Maple fudge for the older kids.. Exhausted and loaded down with packages, I slid onto a metal park bench next to an elderly gentleman.

When he looked at me and smiled and I noticed he appeared to be of Native American decent. He was "small town friendly," immediately spotted me as a tourist, and was eager to chat.

As I leaned forward to organize my many shopping bags, two Native American dolls labeled "Indian Joe" and "Molly" fell to the grass. The old man bend over and picked them up. "I see you found some souvenirs," he said as he carefully studied the two small Indian dolls.

Yes, they are for two of my granddaughters, Madaleine and Olivia, ages six and four."

The old man turned to me, squinted his eyes, and with the two small dolls still in his hands asked, "Do you know who Indian Joe and Molly were?"

"We'll, no," I admitted. I bought them because they were cute and different.

The old man leaned back, looked to the sky and began the story.

In 1745, Indian Joe, then called Sozap by his tribe, was just a little guy, only about six years old. He lived with his family in Louisburg, Nova Scotia when the British attacked, shot his family leaving him an orphan. He was taken in by another Indian family, and hated the British for the rest of his life. During the French and Indian War, Joe, who was then in his teens, was taken on a raid party to Vermont. On one of the attacks near Newbury, Indian Joe was badly wounded and left behind. The colonists were cautious of Indians but Joe was in his teens and very near death, so a white family treated his wounds and nursed him back to health all winter.

Joe grew very close to the family who had helped him. They invited him to stay, but he felt that he belonged with his people. He made a promise to warn the settlers of danger.

While Joe was away he fell in love with a squaw named Molly and stole her and her two infant sons away from another brave.

This gave him the reputation of that of a traitor and a squaw thief. He knew that he could never return.

A Captain in the militia employed Joe as a guide and a General sent him as a Scout on many dangerous missions,. Joe and Molly wandered from place to place. They lived in the little cabin they built, in a makeshift wigwam, a cave and other interesting places.

After the Revolution ended, Indian Joe and Molly received a letter of appreciation from General George Washington. He invited them to his headquarters at Newburgh, New York. Joe and Molly started the trip by canoe and then on foot.

With the Revolution over, Joe and Molly continued to move from place to place, helping people and making many new friends. In 1792, while they were very near the Canadian border, Molly was snatched away from Joe and dragged back by her tribe.

I admit that I was mesmerized by this old man's story.

"Did Joe ever get over losing Molly?" I asked. "What happen to Joe?"

The old man handed the Indian Joe and Molly dolls back to me and I slipped them back into the shopping bag.

"Please continue," I said.

In February 1819, Indian Joe was nearly eighty years old. The sick and deranged old Indian wandered out in the woods after a severe storm and was found there with badly frozen hands and feet.

He died soon after and is buried in old Oxbow Cemetery.

Just then Ken returned.

"Ken, I'd like you to meet this gentleman who just told me the most interesting story," I said.

When I turned to look at the old man he had vanished. I was too stunned to speak.

"Are you alright?" asked Ken.

"We have to find Oxbow Cemetery," I told Ken.

We got in the car and drove ten miles south on I-91 then close to five on William Scott Memorial Highway.

Ken parked the car and we walked together past row after row of grave markers and head stones.

I saw, (and walked over to) a monument labeled General Bayley. Next to it was another that read "Erected in Memory of Old Joe, the Friendly Indian Guide."

"This is it!" I shouted. I went back to the car and got my camera.

Along the way, I picked a bouquet of wild flowers. I placed the flowers at the base of Indian Joe's monument and took a photograph.

I looked up from the camera and there standing along side the Indian's monument was the old man from the park bench. He smiled and waved at me then disappeared again. Ken never saw him.

THE LATE NIGHT HOUSE CALL

A YOUNG HARTFORD PHYSICIAN, a recent Yale graduate, with a promising practice and beautiful bride was looking forward to a good life in the early 1900's. One night, a stranger knocked on the door for help, it was late at night and the doctor's young pretty wife chose to join him rather than stay home alone.

The doctor turned to reassure the stranger that he would indeed do what ever he could to help, but the figure remained in the shadows of the light from he autumn full moon.

A few lamps lit windows along the path down Pratt Street. The doctor's young wife snuggled close in the buggy as the doctor flicked the reins to keep up with the stranger on horseback just a head. They took the Asylum Hill fork in the road. The neighborhood's affluent residents had their large Victorian Gothic, Romanesque, Tudor Revival and Queen Anne style homes brightly lighted,

"Do you think some day we'll be prosperous and prominent? Who are the people who live in these homes?" the doctor's wife asked, as she hugged her new husband's arm.

"The family at this house is active in finance, that one is owned by an importer, my banker lives there and next door is a United States Senator," the young doctor pointed out. Shortly down the street, at the Ambassador to Russia's mansion, the mystery man on his horse led them left onto Farmington Avenue.

"Did you see his old fashioned style of dress?" the doctor's wife asked. "I didn't notice, I couldn't see him well, as he stayed in the dark shadows.. He said his friend is in need of medical treatment. Night calls are always urgent.

The doctor's wife clung to her husband's arm and chattered nervously, "'Farmington Avenue, isn't that where Samuel and Olivia Clemens live? I believe he writes under the pen name of Mark Twain. My friend, Erma told me that Samuel Clemens took a steamship tour of Europe and The Holy Land where he met Charles Langdon. Charles showed Sam a photograph of his sister, Olivia and it was love at first sight,"

They rode deeper into the dark night and now neither one spoke. The shadowy figure and horse turned onto a narrow, gravel side road into the woods. Straining their eyes, they could barely see him dismount. He said nothing; he blended into the shadows as he pointed in the direction of a house.

The young physician whispered to his wife, "Wait for me in the buggy." He deliberately hid his growing uneasiness as he clutched his black medical bag, turned and left. The dry twigs snapped under his shoes as he approached the porch. A single glow in the window directed his way. The front door was ajar, so he entered the dimly-lit parlor. He was not prepared for what he saw. The furniture was over turned, the blood soaked rug, the red splattered walls. The room had a feel as if a violent death had taken place and a body had been dragged across the floor. A trail of blood led to the door of another room. An old man was lying across the bed with a bleeding gash in his arm.

The young doctor's thoughts turned to his wife's safety. He glanced toward the buggy but a voice from the darkness said, "Leave her here!" With his shaking hands, he managed to open his black bag as he bent over the old man.

He treated the wound and bandaged it as quickly as possible. The patient's eyes never glanced away from the doctor' face.

"Your injury isn't as bad as it looks," the doctor tried to hold his trembling voice steady. "Come by my office in the morning and I'll check your arm and change the dressing."

The old man didn't speak but smiled and nodded. Twigs and dry leaves cracked, drew their attention to the window. From the corner of his eye, the doctor got a glimpse of a face, then it was gone.

The young physician turned and made his way back through the bloody room, dodging overturned furniture. Once in the doorway he could see his horse and buggy. It took all the restraint that he could muster not to bolt toward them. He took long steady strides, holding his back straight. Brittle twigs and leaves snapped under every step. An arm, thrust from the darkness and he felt three hard, cold, silver coins slip into his right hand. He slid into the buggy next to his wide eyed trembling wife. The pair, silent the entire ride home, locked the doors and turned on lots of lights. The wife told her husband that she had seen the man waiting in the shadows as well as a man standing on the porch. They decided to call the police, in the morning, when the patient came for his dressing change.

The next day came and went; then three days. Soon a week had passed and the old man had not come to the doctor's office for his follow up examination. When the doctor gave the address to the police he was told it was the address of a restaurant in a park filled with trees and roses. The physician and his wife insisted that the address was correct so two uniformed police officers accompanied them to the address.

There was no mistaking the route. The two remembered every house and turn along the way. They turned down the narrow gravel road and rode trough the trees. There was the house, although it looked different in the daylight. They walked through the door and saw tables set with white linen tablecloths.

"A party of four?" an attractive, well dressed young woman asked, holding a stack of leather bound menu's in her left arm.

"I'm sorry, I believe we've made a mistake," one officer said and the four turned and left the restaurant. Once outside the doctor, his wife and the two police officers were approached by the mysterious stranger from the week before. This time his clothes were covered in blood and he clutched a bloody knife. The officers drew their guns and the man vanished.

No police report was ever made. The doctor maintained patient, doctor confidentiality. The great granddaughter of the physician and his wife, holds in her jewelry box, the three silver dollars which were payment for the treatment that night.

THE MISSING FILE

I WON'T LIE ABOUT it, I had mixed feelings about leaving Memphis. I had never been out of Tennessee before in my life. Daddy had said, "They need good secretaries right here at home." But, I was eager to leave the nest. I decided to take the job offered in "The Insurance Capital of the World," Hartford, Connecticut.

It was 1956 and radios all around me played, Daddy's Little Girl by the Mills Brothers. (which made me emotional) or Heartbreak Hotel by Elvis Presley. I felt homesick but was determined to make it on my own in the Northeast.

Once my accent was identified, the first question was, "Do you know Elvis?" His movie, Love Me Tender, was playing. I discovered that if I simply answered, "We graduated Humes High School together in 1953," and left it at that, it gave me an air of mystic.

I hadn't taken the time or made the effort to make many friends since moving to Connecticut. I found a bedroom to rent in the home of two elderly, maiden sisters in East Hartford. I was quiet, stayed to myself and read all I could about the area, in order to appear to be, "in the know." I spent time alone walking through the Wadsworth Atheneum, the nation's oldest public art museum. I learned that the Hartford Courant is the oldest published newspaper, and across Gold Street from Bushnell Park (the nation's oldest public park) is The Ancient Burial Ground.

It seemed to me that after the two elderly sisters discovered that I didn't want to go there and didn't even like hearing the details of the Ancient Burial Ground, they delighted in bringing up the subject.. They managed to weave some sort of information about it into nearly every conversation, of which I was a part, or within hearing distance.

They told me it was Hartford's first public cemetery and used from 1648 to 1803. "Timothy Stanley is believed to have the oldest gravestone," the old ladies routinely recited. I smiled to myself as I thought of a little joke and wondered what would happen if I asked if, they knew him personally.

The English custom long ago was to place graves randomly in any available spot regardless of family relationship. Grave diggers would probe the soil with rods to determine whether or not a spot was occupied. The newly deceased would be laid to rest once an available area was identified.

Over time, as space became a premium, bodies were buried on top of one another and grave markers became mixed up, destroyed or misplaced.

When the Waverly Building was constructed at the corner of Main and Pearl Streets, several coffins and old bones were dug up.

By the 1890's the cemetery had become terribly neglected. In a determined frenzy, the ladies of The Daughters of the American Revolution took on the project of cleaning up the neighborhood and widening Gold Street, which they referred to it as an alley of slums. If I remember correctly, I think my elderly landlords claimed to be related to one or more of those women involved.

In the process of completing their project, remains of former generations were unearthed. Some were reburied within the cemetery, while sadly, others were carted off to the dump.

Although things got quite stirred up, the cemetery looked much improved, almost beautiful. An iron fence was constructed around Its perimeter, statues of the founding fathers, the Reverends Samuel Stone and Thomas Hooker were added and effort was made to preserve the cemetery and to pay tribute to the 6,000 bodies that were buried there.

In general conversation, I can't tell you how many people asked me if I had visited The Ancient Burial Ground. No, I hadn't and I didn't intend to. It required extensive planning, daily to route myself around Main Street between Gold and Asylum Streets to avoid it.

Then, one rainy morning the heavy fog blocked Main Street at Wells Street. The bus driver stopped directly across the street from the Ancient Burial Ground. Passengers quickly got off the bus and spread, vanishing into the fog. I waited as long as I could, then I got off the bus and walked over next to the iron fence. I stood there wondering how I could reach Bushnell Park while avoiding the cemetery. I was glad I had left the house early that day but if I didn't hurry now, I'd be late for work.

I pulled opened the heavy, black, iron gate. It screeched a rusty song, then closed, slamming behind me. I had changed my mind, turned around and tried to get out, but the gate was jammed. The thick fog made dodging grave markers a challenge. I clutched my

purse and held my file folder close to my chest. I had taken some work home the night before. The ground squished under my feet as though I was walking on a soggy sponge. My focus was on trying to walk toward the voices I heard coming from Bushnell Park. A giant figure blocked my path, He stood directly in front of me; I couldn't move,' I froze. My weak attempt at a scream sounded like a cat choking on a hair ball.

The fog shifted, and I was relieved and felt foolish when I saw that the silent giant was only one of the statues. I couldn't read if it was Samuel Stone or Thomas Hooker. but I saw lights and people in Bushnell park, so I walked a little faster, stood straighter and gripped the bulging file folder. bulging with confidential notes, as well as signed insurance documents.

"Don't be afraid," I thought that I heard a raspy voice. Maybe it was the wind or cracking twigs. Now, my mind must be playing tricks, I thought. "Don't be afraid, you'll be fine," someone had clearly said this time. I saw a hunched over little old man, transparent, as though made of fog. As I turned and started to run, my right arm swung strangely empty.

I had dropped the unlabeled file folder somewhere, but I wasn't going back after it. The spongy ground and the random grave markers slowed me. My pulse throbbing in my ears kept time with

my heart thumping in my chest. My limp legs barely carried me down the sidewalk then up the flight of stairs to the insurance company. I had worked there a full three weeks already. But now I wondered would I be fired for losing the file?

I was out of breath and red faced when I made my way to my desk, weaving between clusters of co-workers chattering about the fog, delays and rerouting. Mindlessly, I went through the routine of pulling out the bottom right desk drawer picking up my coffee mug, and tossing in my purse. I stood up, straightened my pencil skirt and headed toward the coffeemaker.

I passed Mr. Lyon, and I saw him frantically flipping file folders back and forth through the file cabinet He mumbled, "Could it be misfiled?" I just kept walking. My hands shook, spiling a little coffee while filling my mug. I don't remember adding the sugar or pouring the cream. How was I going to explain that I had not only dropped, but then left the unlabeled Buxton file of signed documents in the Ancient Burial Grounds?

As much as I hated the thought, I decided I'd have to go back over to the burial ground and find that file as soon as the fog burned off. Am I just a stupid kid trying to impersonate a responsible adult? I wondered. Carrying my coffee I walked toward my desk. Mr. Lyon had started asking around if anyone had seen the Buxton file. Mr. and Mrs. Buxton were on their way into the office to finalize their insurance policies.

There was no time to go back looking for their file. I'm history, I thought. I imagined myself having to tell my two elderly landlords that I'd been fired. I'd have to move back to Memphis and admit to my parents that I had failed!

When I arrived back at my desk, right there, front and center, just past my chair was an unlabeled file. I looked at the contents, It was the Buxton file. I stood speechless, holding it when Mr. Lyon walked up, took it out of my arms and said, "Great, you found the file for me."

I asked around in the office that day; going as far as to the security guard's log. There was no record of any delivery to our office on that morning.

IN FLEW ENZA, THE GRIZZLY KILLER

IT WAS 1918 in Hartford, Connecticut, and World War I had just passed its fourth anniversary. Civilian life had changed; women and children worked in factories, replacing male workers fighting the war. Beginning in May of 1917, men between the ages of 21 and 29 were required to register for the draft. Soon the draft was expanded to all men between the ages of 18 and 35. Bread, milk, sugar, fruit, tea, textiles, soap and petrol were rationed. and basic food staples were limited. A favorite prank played by a group of boys was to fill an empty sugar bag with sand, set it in plain view, then wait and watch some one take it,

Adding to the difficult situation, that fall an influenza pandemic cut a swath of devastation across all segments of society. Males ages 20 to 40 were significantly affected leaving many young widows and fatherless children.

When school was scheduled to start, elementary school children arrived at St. Joseph's Elementary School only to be turned away and told, "Sorry, you have to go home, the sisters are sick." The school remained closed for three weeks. Soda fountains, theaters and other public places closed to avoid infection.

After about a week of panic, parents all over Hartford lost their battle in keeping the children in the house, isolated from one another. Fear of contracting the flu, sickness and death were becoming their way of life. Hartford's children once again rode their bikes and gathered in groups to play marbles.

Girls skipped well worn, old gray ropes; their long dresses cleared every jump. Hair braids bounced as their black, high top shoes tapped to the rhythm of their sing-song chant. "Bernice saw a bird and named it Enza, she opened the window and in flew Enza. How many others followed Enza? One, two. Three four, five . . . . . .?"

In 1918 the influenza pandemic affected everyone in one way or another. More than 300 people died in Hartford. People became increasingly desperate and aggressive in their demand for treatment. In the town of New Britain, south of Hartford, a man begged a doctor to examine his daughter. The over whelmed physician stated that he had just too many others waiting ahead of them. The father blocked the doctor's Model T Ford, staging a standoff until Mayor Marcus Hensley Holcomb arrived, intervened and arranged for a doctor to treat his child.

The Hartford Golf Club became an emergency medical treatment center as did a ten room house on Asylum Street. Requests for medical assistance came from neighboring states, but the Connecticut Commissioner of Health insisted that all Connecticut physicians and nurses remain in the state and treat their patients.

Because of America's involvement in World War 1, Yale University had been transformed into a military training ground for the Army and Navy, with strict regulations governing the daily life for everyone.

Behind the Gothic gates, the fear of the influenza virus placed Yale campus into a self imposed lock down, a virtual quarantine. Visitors were banned and the university canceled all on-campus public meetings.

Yale's medical resources were supplemented by military on campus and, like New Haven and Hartford had designated buildings as makeshift hospitals to accommodate the increase in patients.

Four friends, members of the Yale University glee club returning from a Barber Shop Quartet competition, and while traveling by train to New Haven, became ill. They vomited, suffered stomach cramp and although they were wet with perspiration and pale in color, they trembled with the chills. The four talented young men got off the train at the Hartford stop. They made it through Bushnell Park, struggling to stay walking upright as boys on bicycles sped past them. The four young men shuffled along, dodging groups of children playing marbles riding bikes and jumping rope.

The girls sang, "Bernice saw a bird and she named it Enza, she opened the window and in flew Enza. How many other birds followed Enza? One, two, three, four, five. . . . . . .they counted until the jumper missed. Then, they would repeat the song.

The four sick men dragged themselves through the hospital doors only to be met by an obstacle course of patients in beds over flowing into the halls. Patients wheezed, whimpered, moaned and coughed convulsively. The vile stench of vomit and excrement not yet attended to, mingled with the odor of disinfectant. Nurse Wilde helped the four students to chairs in a corner, at the end of the hall. There were only two chairs available for the four of them, so two sat on the floor. She gave them water and covered them with blankets hoping a doctor could treat them soon.

In less than twenty-four hours, all four Yale students were dead added the number count to 325 for Hartford, Connecticut.

My great grandfather was a young law professor at Yale University, at the time. For years following the pandemic, as the wind whisk through the campus Elm trees, he heard an indefinable, somber, rendition of a sing-song chant, by male voices in four part harmony. The words to the strange song he heard were unmistakably, "Bernice saw a bird and named it Enza, she opened the window and in flew Enza. How many others?

WHAT IS OLD IS NEW AGAIN AT OLD NEWGATE PRISON

I HAD DRIVEN TO Litchfield County in Connecticut for a week long visit with a former college roommate; but our plans changed for today when he got called into work. Luckily the Colebrook Park and Recreation had an opening on today's day trip. The tour bus turned onto Newgate Road about one-half mile from the intersection of Routes 17 and 20 in East Granby.

One older lady on the bus had been educating us on the history of Old Newgate Prison for the entire ride. At first I listened but then she started to become annoying. She reminded me of the kid who arrives at class early to sit in the front and whose hand flies up before the teacher finishes the question. Maybe she is a retired school teacher, I thought.

"Miss Retired School Teacher," stood in the aisle, facing the back of the bus, holding on with one hand and balancing with her notes in the other. In the beginning she had the attention of all forty- seven passengers as she reported on how in 1705 the prison had originally opened as one of the first commercial mines in the British Colonies. Then, we were on the edge of our seats when she said, "this place has certainly seen its fair share of deaths. When it was operating as a mine, safety conditions were poor. Many miners died within the tunnels from falls and being crushed.

Also, there were many deaths when it was used as a prison, accidents while trying to escape, guards killed inmates, and inmates killed guards and each other."

The bus door opened and we gathered our things, deciding which items to take and which to leave on the seat to save it. Retired school teacher said, "You'll want to take a sweater or light jacket; I've read that the abandoned copper mine/prison is 50 degrees."

As I stepped down out of the bus, the hot Indian Summer sun rode on my shoulders and stung my ears, making 50 degrees sound pretty good. Once inside the Visitor Center, a sign at the gift shop read, "Open to the

Public Fridays, Saturdays and Sundays from May 1st through October 31st."
I noted that the time was approaching to close until spring.

I entered the prison yard through a door on 12' tall walls and looked
around at the remains of prison buildings. If these bricks could talk, I
thought. I shuffled the papers I had picked up in the gift shop and began
to read.

Samuel Higley the owner of the copper mine in 1737 issued three-penny
tokens. He received complaints that they were over-valued so he kept
the Roman numeral three for "3 pence", but changed the legend from "3
pence" to "Value me as you please."

I turned to another brochure and continued to read. John Viets who
ran the tavern across the street in 1773 was approached by the Colonial
Legislature and convinced to turn the old mine into Connecticut's
first prison and to be the prison keeper. At the cost of Three hundred
seventy-five dollars they closed the drain, capped the main shaft with a
heavy iron grill and built a guardhouse over it. They had an escape-proof
prison.

While I was distracted reading the prison yard got quiet; no one else
was around. I walked toward the stairway leading to underground. I felt
the temperature drop with every step. I heard people in the tunnels left
behind by the miners burrowing deep underground. I followed the voices
to an egg shaped, dug out area.

Apparently the group had found a tour guide. I smiled when I saw,
right there, front row and center was "retired school teacher" with her
hand in the air.

I joined the group, and a man from the bus whispered, "This guy is
good! He really plays the part well and knows a lot of detail." I smiled
and nodded, remembering last year when I visited Plymouth Plantation
and Old Sturbridge Village; both places had hired outstanding, period,
costumed, actors as tour guides. This man was as talented an actor, if not
more. I regretted arriving late but was immediately drawn in as he spoke.

"John Hinson, a sly, ornery, elusive character, who could talk his way out of trouble as fast as he found it, was the mine's first prisoner. December 22, 1773 a winter storm dumped two feet of wet, heavy, snow over the entire area. Tree branches broke and the snow fell so fast you couldn't see more than six feet."Collectively the tour group was spellbound as the costumed tour guide continued.

"Prison guard, John Viets closed the tavern and spent the evening in the guardhouse calling comments about the weather, down the shaft. Viets and Hinson debated whether the climate was better on the surface or in the dismal, cavern forty-feet below."

Viets heard a noise which he thought was a breaking tree branch.
He called down the mine shaft to Hinson, but there was no answer.
He unlocked the trap door and with a club and a lantern he descended the forty-foot ladder. Hinson's personal possessions were gone and his bed was empty. Viets frantically searched every inch of the underground tunnels and caverns. His prisoner had escaped.

It was later discovered that a faithful mistress had made her way over snow covered hills, during the blinding snow storm, carrying a 100 foot coil of rope over her shoulder which she let down the well shaft allowing Hinson to escape.

This was the first of many mysterious departures. It seemed that almost as fast as criminals were rounded up and put in the prison, they made a get away. Sometimes prisoners left singly and other times as a group. Guards were doubled, tripled and then quadrupled and still the convicts escaped. It was decided that the prisoners had too many helpful friends and that it was not possible to escape with-out outside assistance.

To stop the escapes once and for all, half-ton boulders were cemented over the top of the well shaft, leaving only a slim slit for ventilation. Over the main entrance a two-story blockhouse was constructed using ten inch timbers. The work was performed using prison labor under armed guard. You guessed it! Every last prison laborer working on the project, somehow slipped away before the roof was put on.

The bus tour group listened intently to their costumed guide's stories.

He continued, "At one point, it was decided that mining should be tried again, using prison labor. The idea was to have the prisoners work under the supervision of a few expert miners. It didn't work. The miners and prisoners became friends and the mining picks and shovels became useful tools for escape One prisoner escaped while being carried out after he substituted his body for that of a corpse.

We, I mean they were provided musty straw, crawling with vermin, on which to sleep and thrown half-edible pickled pork at noon and corn meal mush for the evening meal every day ;.year after year. Between 1773 and 1775 practically every prisoner managed to escape one way or another or died trying."

The bus lady's hand went up.

"Were there any women prisoners here?" she asked.

"Yes Mame, there were four," the tour guide responded,
"Juli Ann Burr and Comfort Sperry were both serving time for adultery, Rachel Heddy for stealing and Thirza Mansfield was sentenced to life in here for killing her husband."

"Are there any other questions?"

Another hand went up and a gentleman from the bus asked,
"Where were the prisoner's restrooms?"
"The prisoners used buckets and the job of the cullyman was to collect and empty them.

Before you go back to the bus, I want to tell you about one last prisoner named "Starkey". They were twenty-four hours away from moving the prisoners to a clean, modern institution in Wethersfield. Sociologists started testing a new theory that prisoners might be reformed by making them more comfortable and by using less stern discipline. The night before the move, Starkey climbed hand over hand up an old frayed rope. When he reached the top, the old rope snapped and he plunged to his death."

The "retired school teacher" spoke for the entire group. "Thank you very much for all the wonderful information and interesting stories. We didn't get your name."

"Just call me Adam"

"Thank you, Adam. Good bye".

The group climbed out of the copper mine/prison and boarded the bus. I paused for a moment and told the greeter we appreciated the well informed, costumed, tour guide down in the mining cavern.
He told us stories with great passion.

Looking puzzled, the greeter answered, "We don't have any tour guides."

Later, during the ride back, I read in one of the pamphlets I bought in the gift shop that the last prisoner to die trying to escape was Adam Starkey.

SHERLOCK'S HOME
White Tulips at Gillette Castle

WILLIAM GILLETTE KNEW he was going to be an actor even though his parents frowned on his choice, expecting him to be a lawyer or a statesman. He was meticulous, eccentric, and at the same time displayed a manly demeanor. He grew up on Nook Farm with, talented and interesting, literary, intellectuals such as Harriet Beecher Stowe, Mark Twain and Charles Dudley as neighbors. Twain cast young Gillette in his play, The Gilded Age, to give him a start and some experience.

Gillette figured he could make the most money in the triple role of playwright, director and actor. In 1881, the Frohman brothers, Gustave and Daniel hired him to write, direct and act for $50 per week.

The first play he wrote and produced, The Professor, debuted in the Madison Square Theater, near Broadway at 24th Street, behind the Fifth Avenue Hotel, in New York City. The play was performed 151 times before it went on tour.

Gillette, a fashion conscious, matinee idol with his aristocratic, six foot three inches tall, well-proportioned frame, stood strong and dignified. He acted in a contemporary style, carefully calculating every gesture and subtle mannerism for effect. In his private life Gillette was alone, concealed his emotions, acted aloof and lived a quiet, free of scandal life. During a Detroit performance, of The Professor, he spotted the beautiful, twenty-one years old, Helen Nichols, seated in the audience. He arranged to meet her, then uncharacteristically for him, he presented her with a bouquet of white French tulips. She was deeply touched; and that was when he learned that white tulips were her favorite.

The two were a perfect match. She was sweet, genteel, and a true lady. They shared the same interests, were warm and loving companions. She flourished in the social skills he often lacked.

Following a brief courtship they were married June 1, 1882, in an intimate, elegant, ceremony in Windsor, Ontario, Canada. Helen, an only child, appeared for the ceremony in a beautiful gown which had been worn by her mother. The high neck, long sleeve, ivory satin gown was adorned with imported lace and crystal. beads. Her groom presented her with a huge bouquet to carry, of white hydrangea, white calla lilies and white French tulips.

Helen loved traveling with her husband as his play, The Private Secretary toured the country. Being childless, they shared an idyllic, undistracted, devotion to one another.

In June they celebrated their sixth wedding anniversary in Greenwich, Connecticut. By late August, Helen began to complained of painful abdominal attacks and on September 1, 1888 she died from peritonitis, caused by a ruptured appendix. Gillette was devastated by the loss.

Had it happened a little later, she could have been saved. The following year, the medical community released early diagnostic symptoms for appendicitis, then in 1893 the removal of the inflamed portion surgically was described.

Grief-stricken Gillette never totally got over losing his Helen. He didn't act for years and he never remarried.

Despondent, he moved to Tyron, North Carolina, where he built a cabin he named Thousand Pines. Among the stately, green pines randomly grew, dainty delicate, wild, white tulips.

When he returned to work, he finished what was said to be his best play, Secret Service also considered to be the best of many Civil War plays produced after the war.

Gillette developed the character, Sherlock Holmes, while helping Sir Arthur Conan Doyle with adaptations to the play. Secret Service was still playing in San Francisco and Gillette stayed at the Palace Hotel while his secretary, William Postance, (with possession of the Sherlock Holmes' script) stayed at the Baldwin Hotel. Around 3:30 in the morning on November 23, a fire swept throughout the Baldwin, reducing the entire script to ashes. Postance escaped unharmed and Gillette rewrote the play in a month.

Gillette threw himself into the portrayal of Sherlock Holmes, as a brave, open to express his feelings, deerstalker cap wearing, cape wearing, bent briar pipe smoking, sleuth. Props such as a magnifying glass, a violin and a syringe also became part of Sherlock Holmes. In his lifetime, Gillette played the part approximately 1,300 times for both American and English audiences.

He said that he always felt Helen's presence with him. A bouquet of white tulips mysteriously appeared in his dressing room after performance.

Gillette created the image of Sherlock Holmes so real that many believed the detective really lived. The first time that he tried to retire was shortly after he purchased his 144 foot, 200 ton houseboat, "Aunt Polly". For the five years of construction of his retirement dream house, he divided his time between living at his home in Greenport, Long Island and on his houseboat. He announced his retirement many times throughout his career but retirement didn't actually happen until his death in 1937 at the age of eighty-three.

In 1910, while sailing on Long Island Sound, trying to escape reality, he turned the wheel on a whim and headed up the Connecticut River. Gillette spotted a hill, part of the Seven Sister's chain. He docked that evening then climbed up 200 feet to the top and fell in love with the amazing view. One month later he purchased 115 acres of the land overlooking the Connecticut River.

His "retirement home" masterpiece, Gillette Castle, remains to this day. although he did not refer to it as a castle, his neighbors did. It got back to him that people referred to his home as "Hadlyme Stone Heap," "The Rock Pile," and "Gillette's Folly."

Gillette was fascinated with exotic aesthetics. The house and the grounds were designed to the smallest detail, by Gillette himself with his eye for detail and his dramatic flare.

Gillette designed the aerial trolly to carry building materials up to the site The house has 24 rooms, the main room being 30 feet by 50 feet and 19 feet high. The 47 unique and elaborate doors have hand carved puzzles levers, some fashioned after backstage theater levers while others look like steam locomotive levers,. They took a ship's carpenter a year to construct.

The castle's granite walls tapered from 5 feet thick at the base to 3 feet thick at the tower. A mirrored surveillance system of the public rooms transmit to his bedroom. The dramatic Gillette once explained this as a means to "make a great entrance at the opportune moment". His personal quarters, a bit more dramatically decorated than the rest of the house, featured Japanese floral embellishments with a light-switching system designed to be operated from the bed.

The cellar is approximately twelve feet deep and was blasted out of solid rock. Despite the castle's appearance, it is steel framed. The field stone was gathered from the river bed by local farmers for one dollar a cartload.

The mansion was finished in 1919 at a cost of one million dollars. He shared his home with a school of goldfish, pet frogs and 15 cats. Gillette had installed, three miles of train track on the grounds which he called the Seven Sisters shoreline. He once treated Albert Einstein, Helen Hayes and Charlie Chapman to a terrifying train ride along the edge of the cliff.

Gillette also enjoyed strolls around the property with the former U.S. President Calvin Coolidge and the former Mayor of Tokyo Ozaki Yukio.

His final appearance on stage as Sherlock Holmes, took place on March 19, 1932, in Wilmington Delaware. On April 29, 1937, he died due to a pulmonary hemorrhage and was buried in the Hooker family plot at Riverside Cemetery, Farmington, Hartford County, Connecticut, next to Helen, the love of his life. Around both headstones, wild white tulips grow, without having been planted.

From where did the mysterious white tulips come during all those years?

"Elementary, my dear Watson."

THE SECRETS

RING "HELLO"
ANSWERED DARLENE
while wiping a little dust off the telephone table, using the hem of her apron.

"I'm pregnant!" her thirty-one year old daughter, Janice was ecstatic. Janice and her husband had just celebrated their eighth wedding anniversary, but to Janice it had meant, marking another childless year of trying to start a family.

"But, Mom, don't tell anyone yet, OK? We want to wait a while before we tell people this time."

Darlene could feel the emotional roller coaster start climbing.
Janice and John had false alarms and heartbreaking miscarriages over the years. Seeing pregnant women, and mothers with babies became more painful every day. The couple watched their friends started families, several by now expecting their second and third little additions.

Darlene was keeping another family secret. Janice's younger brother Jason and his bride, Katherine married just six months were three months pregnant, too.

It was times like this that Darlene especially missed her own parents, who died more than thirty-two years ago, before they were able to enjoy grandparenthood. Darlene and Jim made a deliberate point of speaking often of Darlene's parents to their children, Janice and Jason, as they were growing up. The grandparents' photographs were displayed in their home and they shared amusing old family stories with the kids to make their late grandparents real to them. During Janice's and Jason's growing up years, even a few amusing, individual personality idiosyncrasies similar to Grandpa's, surfaced.

Today, Darlene was thrilled at the prospect of becoming a grandmother not once, but now twice. She guarded her emotions and tried hard not to worry that there would be disappointments with the pregnancies. Today she especially missed her long time deceased parents.

Weeds had started taking over in her flower garden. She bent over and pulled on a tall weed. The rain last night let it easily slide from the soil's grasp. Darlene, deep in thought, pulled weeds one by one. She couldn't get her parents off her mind. They'd be so proud of their grandchildren and their soon to be great grandchildren

Darlene piled the weeds to dry and located her wicker gathering basket. It had been a longtime since she'd gone to Glenwood cemetery.

Today she would take flowers to her parent's graves. Rose pink peonies, royal blue iris with yellow throats and white Shasta daisies made strikingly colorful bouquets. She cut some fern and long ivy, then located her metal cemetery vases. They were especially designed to be set on the ground and had long sharp prongs on the bottom to secure them in the earth.

Darlene tossed everything, along with a plastic jug of water, into the bed of the old red pick up truck. She headed toward Pleasant Street, turned left on Farman Avenue then right on US 48 and left onto Old Pint Tree Road. She didn't know why she hadn't visited her parents' graves more often over the past thirty plus years since they died. Maybe it was because, although she thought of her parents she didn't think of them in the grave but pictured them shuttling between heaven and at her side, guiding her in daily decisions.

Darlene drove past rows of headstones bearing familiar family names. Almost everyone she knew had relatives buried in this cemetery. She had noticed throughout the years, from the street, while driving past, that some of the family plots were extensively decorated, changing every season and holiday. She passed one headstone anchoring a blue balloon that read "Happy Birthday" on it. Clearly, there were people who visited the graves of their loved ones often.

Off in the distance to her left, she saw a new grave mounded with wilting fresh flowers. Her heart broke again as she was reminded of the raw pain accompanying the death of a family member.

Looking around she saw that graves were adorned with blooming, growing plants, fresh flowers in metal cemetery vases similar to those she had brought with her today. Several tall headstones sported stoles of artificial flowers secured with metal clamps.

There were those graves too, like her parent's that were well groomed and maintained by a cemetery worker, but remained undecorated.

Darlene wondered if she would remember the location of her parents' graves, then surprised herself when she stopped the truck, got out and walked right to the spot. Seeing their names etched in stone, even though they left this earth decades ago, underscored the reality. Darlene sat on the dry grass between the two graves. She looked around and saw that she was the only person in the cemetery.

"Mom and Dad. I haven't come before because of the sadness and pain of losing you. I feel your presence every day and believe that you somehow still advise and guide our family," she said aloud.

Darlene, glanced around, surveying the cemetery, determining that she was still alone there.

"Mom and Dad, Jim and I have two children, they're grown now, ages thirty-one and twenty-five and both married to wonderful people. But, I know you know that. I sense you with me and know you are watch over us.

Janice and John have been married for eight years now and have suffered a lot of pain and heartache in trying to start a family, but you know that, too," Darlene said aloud, by now without concern of whether or not anyone would hear her.

Darlene sat in the sun, on the grass, between her parent's graves and chatted and laughed as though they were together in a house or restaurant. They had died unexpectedly and too young.

"Janice was born the year after you died," She told them. "Jason came along six years after his sister. They both graduated Dartmouth College in Hanover, they have good jobs and are happily married. You would be so proud of them. Mom, Janice has been wearing your beautiful, unique wedding band on her right hand since her twelfth birthday." Darlene paused as though expecting a response, then she realized she had been talking to grave stones a good part of the afternoon. She added the last of the water to the fresh flowers that she had brought, gathered her things and put everything in the truck.

Her eyes scanned the entire cemetery. She decided she would stop at a plant nursery before next time and bring some growing plants for the base of the grave stones. Maybe she would decorate in the fall and then for Christmas too. To Darlene's surprise the visit to her parent's graves had felt natural and comforting.

The next morning, Darlene and Jim started their day, early as usual. Before they retired from working, they longed to sleep late, never dreaming that they would now enjoy rising before the sun. It had become their routine; chatting as they wondered in their backyard, talking while pulling a weed here and there. Every morning presented a treasure missed by those still sleeping. Colors shoot across the sky; sometimes, pink and purple and other times yellow and orange just before the bright yellow sun peeks out. They lost track of the time until the growl in their stomach drew them into the kitchen for breakfast. The phone was ringing when they walked into the kitchen through the back door.

"Hello," Darlene answered.

"Hi Mom," Jason said, "I had the oddest dream last night. Grandpa was alive and came over to the house. He was talking as though our baby was already born and mentioned a fishing buddy cousin, Janice's son. It has been years since I had a dream with grandpa in it."

Darlene and her son continued to talk about other things while Jim started the pancakes. While they were eating, the phone rang again.

"Hello," Darlene answered.

"Mom, everything is going to be alright this time," Janice said. " I had the most beautiful dream – I didn't want to wake up. Grandma held my hand and told me how proud she was that I wear her ring and keep her near. She patted my belly and said your son will grow into a fine young man and be best friends with his cousin, Jason's boy.

ERMA'S RECIPE

"I WISH WE HAD Grandma Erma's sugar cookie recipe for these, complained Lucy. These are alright but I remember her's were fabulous.

"That was a long time ago, and as little girls we thought anything Grandma made was fabulous. In fact, back then we thought all cookies were fabulous.

Another family tradition was the Farmer's Market, during the summer in beautiful Colburn Park and in the winter over at the Lebanon United Methodist Church. If Grandma wasn't selling vegetables, eggs, cheese or baked goods, then she was there buying hand made pottery and listening to the music. Performers from New Hampshire and Vermont would entertain.

What a sense of humor Grandma Erma had, even when she knew that she wouldn't get well. When Mom went through Grandma's things she found a note in this cookbook saying, "this is the recipe you're looking for." It was that tricky chocolate cake she put together warm with marshmallow between the layers. "She would never give it to me," Lucy said, as she fanned the pages of an old, well worn cookbook.

"The cookie recipe probably isn't even written anywhere. I remember Grandma cooking or baking and when I'd ask for the recipe she'd say, "oh, just a pinch of this, a dab of that, a fist full of flour and a pat o butter the size of a walnut." The cookie recipe probably went to Glenwood Cemetery with her" I placed the mixing bowels ,mixing spoons, measuring cups and measuring spoons in the sink, then turned on the hot water. I grabbed a dish cloth, held it under the faucet, twisted out the water and wiped down the counter top. My eyes spotted familiar handwriting; it was Grandma Erma's beautiful penmanship. I haven't seen it in decades.

"They don't emphasize writing like this in school these days. Penmanship at this level is a lost art." I said.

"Lucy, where did this come from?"

"what is it?"

"The long lost, fabulous cookie recipe that we talked about earlier and have never been able to find. Here it is, in Grandma's handwriting," I answered, as I flipped over the page.

"How can this be?" Lucy looked shocked. " It was the back side is a calendar."

"It is last month's page which I tore off and threw in the trash this morning just before you arrived."

Erma's Recipe

Cut Out Sugar Cookies

1 ½ cups sifted confectioner sugar

1 cup butter, 1 egg, 1 teaspoon vanilla

2 ½ cups sifted all purpose flour

1 teaspoon cream of tartar

1 teaspoon soda

Cream sugar and butter, add egg and flavorings, mix thoroughly. Sift dry ingredients together and stir in. Heat oven to 375 degrees. Divide dough in half then roll out on a lightly floured pastry sheet. Roll out thin but thick enough to pick up the design in the cookie cutters. Dip the cookie cutters in flour before each cutting. Cut as many cookies from each rolling as possible, as the least amount of working with the dough, gives the best cookie. Place on lightly greased baking sheet and bake for 7 or 8 minutes.

THE LONG WAY TO
THE HAUNTED FOREST

IN THE MID 1950's Dad was in the prime of his career, when he made an announcement that changed all of our lives. It didn't matter that my sister and I were rooted and thriving in America's heartland. In fact the move to the East coast was a cultural shock to the whole family. None of us were much aware of any life beyond the Midwest, flat, farmland of corn, wheat and soybeans before Dad's promotion.

I didn't hear much of what dad had said that night beyond it being the opportunity of a lifetime for him to research new products in the insurance industry, in the insurance capital. My thoughts tuned in and out as he said something about selling the house, relocating 900 miles east, being close to New York City and a new school.

Four months later we moved into the new house, in a new neighborhood, in a new state. Although it wasn't as bad as I'd feared, I did feel that I must have been invisible during the lunch break; one of the first days at the new school. Fortunately, I had read about the area before the move when I asked, "Have you guys heard of a haunted forest somewhere in Connecticut?"

That one question broke the ice and I was drawn into the group. You're talking about Dudleytown. It is an extinct settlement that some call a ghost town or haunted forest. Years ago my father and his buddies went there as kids and saw all sorts of neat foundations and things. They climbed a few high hills and rocks to look all around. They were fascinated then and mention it even now. There was and is no sign of any living thing there. They did not even see a squirrel near the trees. They said that when you walk in where the town stood, you can actually feel uneasy vibes that give you the worst case of goose bumps ever. Just hearing Dad talk about it gives me a rush. He remembers that the rocks were smooth and shiny, like glass with a greenish blue tint to them. But don't take any; don't even touch them! I heard that a dude took a hand full and died in a car crash a week later. I plan to go up this fall, with Hank, a good friend of mine. Dad thinks the place is haunted, but as long as you don't do anything stupid, then nothing will happen to you.

A girl named, Myrna added, "I did a whole research project on The Haunted Forest for Mr. Edwards in the 8th grade. I found information back to England in 1510. Edmund Dudley was beheaded and a curse was put on the Dudleys for plotting to overthrow King Henry VIII. Robert Dudley left England to avoid losing his own head. William Dudley Sr. was born in Richmond, Surrey, England in 1608. William Dudley, II, was born aboard a ship headed for America in 1639. His son, Joseph was born in Saybrook, Connecticut in 1674 and had twelve children. During the 1740's some of Joseph Dudley's descendents; (the names, Gideon, Abijah, Barzillai, Abiel and Martin come to my mind, but it's been a while since 8th grade) bought land in the Appalachian Mountains between: The Coltsfoot Triplets, Bald Mountain and Woodbury Mountain. The location is known by several different names, The Haunted Forest, Dark Entry, Owlsbury and Dudleytown.

The farmers grew rye, flax, wheat, corn and other foods there, then dammed up streams to supply power for at least three mills. The ruins are still visible today. The town was so isolated that when there was a death, they couldn't bury their dead until an ox cart could carry the body down the mountain to the Cornwall cemeteries. The first recorded death occurred in 1792, when during a barn raising, when a man fell, or was shoved, from an unfinished barn structure and died.

An odd thing happened. The man who bought Abiel's house felt something was wrong with the town so he moved his family away. His son Nathan was left behind and the only lucky member of the family when in October 1764 mother, baby, and father were killed by Indians and the three remaining children taken captive. His brother and his family then died of a cholera epidemic. In 1804, a lady was struck and killed by lightening during a spring storm.

Horace Greeley married Mary Cheney, a Dudleytown resident who was born in Dudleytown and died a violent death there. Mrs. Greeley hung herself in 1872, just one week before her husband lost his bid for the presidency of the United States.

A guy named Alex set his lunch tray down and joined the discussion. "Talking about Dudleytown? I know some guy's brother who went up there looking around once .The car started acting strangely when they pulled up Bald Mountain Road. just before they parked at the entrance of one of the over grown trails. The car died right in front of a NO TRESPASSING sign. They grabbed their flashlights, cameras and jumped out of the car, walked a few yards and immediately felt a chill. There was dead silence, no wind, birds, or chipmunks. A while later, the earth beneath them shifted and they heard a moan. One guy said it wasn't a moan but a voice saying, "get out!" The group freaked and scurried back to the car. A Connecticut State Police Officer waited for them next to the NO TRESPASSING sign. The group gladly paid the $75.00 fine each plus a towing charge to get out of there. They pledged to never speak of it to anyone but then the police log was published in the newspaper.

What was the population of the town and what happened to the last family?" I asked. Everyone spoke at once and different numbers were given, but all were in the range of 25 families and 100 people.

" The last residents were the John Patrick Brophy family. At the end of the 1800's Mrs. Brophy died of consumption and their two children mysteriously disappeared in the woods. After the home burned to the ground, John Brophy walked away from Dudleytown never to be seen again." said a newcomer to the lunch table.

Later that night, at dinner, Dad tried to answer the Dudleytown mysteries. "Let's think about this," he said. "A crop produced at Dudleytown was rye, used to make bread. If it goes bad, the mold is almost a hallucinogen and makes you see things and it could kill you. Then there are the old foundations, root cellars, stone fences causing a rocky terrain, concealed by moss and grass creating dangerous obstacles, pits and traps, the locals call, fairy caves." One wrong move and your foot could get stuck, twisted, cut or broken. The fairy caves could be to blame for the missing people and animals. Their drinking water could have contained high levels of iron and other metals. I'm guessing that the shadow from three mountains probably didn't allow much sunlight causing mold, moss and acidic soil. This makes more sense to me than curses and ghosts.

"So, Dad, you don't sound as though you think the forest is haunted," I said. "Does that mean I can go check it out?"

"I don't believe that the forest is haunted but that doesn't mean that I'm giving you permission to go, nor do I think it is dangerous. If you are careful, I'm not banning you from there either," he said.

He seemed interested enough to me to go too if he were invited. Back at school, my new friends didn't let the subject of ghosts and haunted places die down. Tim, was first in our group to get his driver's license, and time was not wasted in planning a ride to Dudleytown.

"Let's start our haunted hunt with lunch in Simsbury," Myrna invited herself. There is a restaurant there that everybody knows is haunted. It was built in 1780 for the son of a patriot killed near New York in 1776 during The Revolution. It was a stagecoach stop on the Hartford to Boston route on the Albany Turnpike."

A red headed kid slid his chair to the table and added, "I heard it was used by Captain Phelps to plan with Ethan Allen and the Green Mountain Boys, the capture of Fort Ticonderoga in New York.

"Remember when Miss Rogers told us the first two presidents stopped there during their travels? I didn't really believe it but later learned that George Washington is mentioned by name in a US Supreme Court case involving the restaurant regarding the quartering of troops. John Adams' memoirs say that he preferred the Albany Turnpike to the Boston Post road that runs along the shoreline of Connecticut. He traveled it from his farm in Quincy, Massachusetts to the Continental Congresses in Philadelphia and to New York, both as vice president and as president."

"How do you know all this?" I asked.

"There has been a lot written about the ghosts in this area," Myrna answered. "The restaurant was burned to the ground by Indians in 1800 then rebuilt and opened a few years later.

Everybody around here knows someone who has worked there and the employees all say the same thing. The spirit's name is Abigail.. Her husband returned early from a whaling trip and caught her in the arms of a local man. The enraged sailor used an axe to kill both Abigail and her lover. For a long time the huge disgrace of an adulteress and a murder in the puritan, colonial New England was not spoken of. Then, playful, childlike Abigail let herself be known. Employees and guests alike can attest to being called by name in a familiar voice but turn around to realize that there is no one there.

Several closing managers have told of someone or something playing with the lights and music, and of leaving the dark building only to realize as they pull out of the parking lot that all the lights are back on.

Opening managers have come in the morning to find furniture stacked up or rearranged. One opening manager arrived to find one of the nearly indestructible, solid oak chairs smashed to pieces in the middle of the dining room; a difficult task for a mortal.

Most of this activity occurs late at night under a full moon or early in the morning. Female customers repeatedly report seeing the reflection of a beautiful, young, eighteenth century woman in the mirror of the ladies room instead of her own reflection.

"When do we go?" I asked.

The next full moon is Saturday, October 1" answered

Tim, was the kid with the driver's license; So, the plan was hatched that Tim, Myrna, Alex and I would eat in Simsbury, then drive to Cornwall and see what we could find in Dudleytown.

The restaurant in Simsbury was fancier than a watering hole for high school kids. It was more a place you'd go for dinner on prom night or where your parents would take you on your birthday or they'd go on their anniversary.

From the moment we crossed the threshold, the four of us were on the lookout for Abigail. We watched our plates and silverware. We studied the lights, chairs and other customers. Myrna went unto the lady's room, looked into the mirror and called for Abigail. There was no sign of her.

I've since heard that the playful spirit won't be summoned but only appears or performs at her own will.

We left the restaurant in Simsbury, feeling a little disappointed. Tim turned onto Hopmeadow Road and drove toward Albany Turnpike.

"Let's go to the Seventh Day Baptist Cemetery and find the Green Lady."

"Is the cemetery on the way?"

"It can be," Tim said. "with a left on Elm for around ten miles, a left onto cemetery Road and a sharp left onto Pine and we're in Burlington."

People have reported The Green Lady making her appearance in the graveyard for more than 100 years.

In the early 1800s some residents of Burlington weren't very happy when so many religious "Sabbatarians" of the Seventh Day Baptist Church, migrated to their neighborhood. One after another, accidents appeared to be picking off the newcomers. One was killed when a tree fell on him in the woods, another accidently was hung while repairing a lamp, a man fell from his ladder while fixing his roof and a recently finished roof fell in on another. It can't be agreed upon if these were all coincidence or intimidation by the locals trying to get them to leave.

The remaining members moved to Brookfield, New York in 1820. But, before they moved, Elizabeth, the Green Lady, died in April 1800.

There was a late blizzard that year and her husband, Benjamin left during the storm to get supplies. Once in town, he was unable to return home that night. The next day, when he did return, Elizabeth was missing. Apparently, she worried when he had not returned, had gone out searching for him and became lost. An exhausting search ended when her drowned, frozen body was found in the swamp.

The Green Lady is not, threatening, harmful or menacing. She just appears as a green mist of human, female form with happy, smiling, feminine facial features.

I thought we had all agreed to stay in Tim's car and slowly drive past the cemetery. The car stopped on a slight incline.

"Why are we stopping?" I asked. But, before Tim answered, the car's motor turned off.

"It's doing it by it's self, I didn't stop."

After sitting in the car, unable to go anywhere, Tim and Alex opened their doors and got out.

"What are you doing?"

Not wanting to either get out of the car or to stay in it either, Myrna and I reluctantly got out too. The four of us were standing about twenty feet in front of Tim's car when it rolled up hill as though someone was pushing it.

My instinct was to run in the opposite direction but the others ran toward the car and got in, so I did too. The car started right up but a thin frost covered the windshield. It turned from white to green and formed the face of a smiling lady.

We didn't continue on to Dudleytown. In fact, we didn't mention our Green Lady experience, or talk about it even to each other, until years later at our ten year class reunion.

OLD LEATHER MAN'S GHOST

MY GRANDMOTHER AND great uncle Otis, (my grandmother's brother), both told our family the same version of the story I am about to share with you. It was March 20, 1939 and they were visiting a relative in Thomaston, Connecticut, playing in what was called a cave. Since they had been both instructed and warned to stay away from caves, they emphatically explained in detail that it was a stone shelter, formed from rock broken away from a cliff located above. The large rock chunks and slabs formed the ceiling and walls making it a great place to play.

On one of several visits to this rock formation, which turned out to be their last, they saw an old man dressed in an odd patchwork leather costume, sitting next to a fire. The kids stood silently watching him for a few minutes but when he saw them, the old man as well as his campfire vanished. The two hysterical kids raced back, convinced and screaming that they had just seen a ghost.

They were told about a wanderer who dressed in a crude leather suit, arousing curiosity and fear. When he first appeared in Connecticut as a young man in1856 some residents threw stones and rotted vegetables at him, but as time passed, they came to expect his appearances in their towns. He took the tobacco from cigarette and cigar butts he retrieved from the ground, or from people in town, then smoked it in a pipe that he had designed himself. As time passed, and the townspeople got to know him, and fear him less, they came to responded to his simple requests and supplied him with food, leather scraps, tobacco and money. Over time they offered their homes to the Leatherman and it became an honor to feed him. He walked a clockwise circuit of 365 miles every 34 days between the Connecticut and Hudson Rivers. He traveled in a clockwise direction, never once retracing his steps. From Harwinton his route took him to Bristol, Forestville, Southington, Kensington, Berlin, Middletown and south along the west side of the Connecticut River to the shore towns, then west to Westchester County in New York state . Without crossing the Hudson, he turned east into Connecticut near Ball's Pond. From Danbury he went north to New Milford, to Roxbury, Woodbury, Watertown, Plymouth and back to Harwinton, thus completing his cycle. Prominent citizens were known to have missed church socials if they knew he was going to come through town.

No one knows for certain who he was, but for a while it was thought that he was from Lyons, France. The story is that he met and fell in love with the daughter of a leather merchant, but he was a wood carver and therefore of a lower social level. The girl's father objected to the match, but the French girl persuaded her father to bring him into the family's leather firm. Her father said that only on the condition that he made good, would his daughter ever become his bride.

The young Frenchman worked very hard and proved to be worthy and a good addition to the firm. He earned promotion after promotion taking on greater responsibilities. When he became a purchaser of leather the bride's father gave them his blessing and the young couple set their wedding date. Before the 1855 wedding took place, the price of leather dropped about forty per cent overnight and he overbought in stock. His future father's in-law leather firm, was destroyed and he had brought ruin on himself and those he loved. Distraught, he was found wandering the streets of Lyon when he was placed under the care of a physician. Two years later he disappeared and was never seen again in France.

About this same time a man was seen walking through the town of Harwinton, Connecticut wearing an outfit, from his cap to his boots made of leather patches. A month later the man returned. Who was he? One bold lady inquired. and when she did not get a response, the stranger became known as, "The Leather Man."

The Leather Man never wore out his welcome because he only asked for one meal in thirty-four days from any household. He had more people concerned about his food, his health and his comfort than anyone else in Connecticut. He made his tools which he carried in a leather bag, which he also made. He repaired his outfit with patches of leather and sometimes did his own cooking. Some say that he chose to dress in leather because it was the material that brought about his ruin. It is more likely that he decided on his attire because leather was in common use and could be had for the asking.

The leather kept him dry because it shed rain like no other material and when an area wore out it was replaced by another easily found patch. It may have been cumbersome and maybe a little too heavy for all season comfort and use, but it was the best he had.

Every town he passed through had at least one tannery and today each of these towns has its own Leather Man's cave. The Leather Man era covered almost a third of a century. It began before Lincoln was president and continued until 1889. To some he appeared to be walking all the time when in fact, he traveled only about ten miles a day, taking ample time for rest and refreshment. The Leather Man was pointed out to children who grew up, married, had families of their own and in turn pointed him out to their children. He became know as the "old" Leather Man because it seemed as if he traveled on forever. In time, and the weight of years and weather was noticeable.

He was so regular in his travels that people knew the very day to expect him; the exact hour and almost the exact minute. It was said "housewives set their clocks by him." The Leather Man could not have known the effect he had on the lives of people that adjusted their activities to his whims. He never accepted an invitation to sleep indoors, regardless of the inclement weather but made himself comfortable through his own ingenuity and handicraft.

Before leaving his cave each day an inverted "v" of small dry sticks would be placed in the center of his shelter, needing only to be lighted on his next arrival. He stored dry wood in the rock crevices within the cave. Because of his preparation, little time was lost in starting a fire after a day's journey and soon the small area was comfortable and warm. When enough coals had accumulated to warm the hearth thoroughly, they were swept outside and the Leather man lay down to sleep on a warm stone bed. It was sufficiently warm for him to come through every winter.

The Leatherman became a beloved character. Ten towns along the Leatherman's route passed ordinances exempting him from the state "tramp law" passed in 1879. He was fluent in French but he communicated mostly with grunts and gestures. It is unknown how he earned his money, although one store kept a record of his order, "one loaf of bread, a can of sardines, one-pound of fancy crackers, a pie, two quarts of coffee, one gill (4 oz.) of brandy and a bottle of beer."

He declined meat on Fridays causing speculation that he might be Roman Catholic. The humane society had him arrested one time in Middletown, Connecticut in 1888 to examine and treat a sore on his lip. He was diagnosed at Hartford Hospital with cancer of the lip and jaw. While people were unsure about what to do with him, he disappeared before being treated.

The Leatherman died March 20, 1889 of blood poisoning from cancer, which is believed to have been caused by his tobacco use. His body was discovered March 24, 1889 in his Saw Mill Woods cave near Ossining, New York. A French language prayer book was found on his body.

TROMPE L'OEIL
DECEIVE THE EYE

TROMPE L'OEIL IS an ancient art technique involving extremely realistic imagery in order to create optical illusions. Italian painters of the 1450's used perspective techniques such as foreshortening in order to give the impression of greater space to the viewer below. The elements above are treated as if viewed from the true vanishing point perspective.

Chuck and Billy were two young, artists, roommates, art academy classmates and friends who shared studio space as well.

They playfully explored the artistic boundary between image and reality.

The friends toured Europe one semester to study large Trompe L'Oreal style murals painted on the sides of city buildings in Germany. From there, their curiosity led them to churches in Rome where ceilings were painted to optically open to the heavens. The more of this art style the two saw, the more it provoked their competitive, creative natures. When back home in Vermont, they both painted exclusively manipulating and disrupting perspective to appear to project the images into the viewer's space.

It became a serious duel of the artists. Billy painted a still life allowing a nail head to appear to protrude into the viewer's real space.

Chuck painted an ice cold, frosted mug of lemonade, balancing a slice of yellow lemon wedge on the lip of the glass. He pained a bluish black horse fly which appeared to be hydrating from the swollen lemon membrane.

Billy painted an open window with an ocean view and the illusion of unbleached, gauze curtains blowing in the breeze. Chuck came back with an entire beach scene, covering two walls from floor to ceiling. Seagulls appeared to fly off the canvas and white foam waves teased the viewer.

Chuck was once terribly embarrassed when he was fooled by one of Billy's paintings. Upon entering the grand ballroom of a hotel he was visiting, he caught a glimpse of a beautiful woman descending a stair into the room. Chuck is said to have greeted the woman before he realized he was talking to a canvas painted by Billy.

Both men continued to perfect their art of blurring the boundaries between real and represented. The two artists were no longer enjoying the mutual interest and love for art. Their passion for creativity had sadly developed into a fierce competition that destroyed their friendship.

Billy and Chuck went their separate ways, both continued to develop and fine tune their art. They separately painted for churches, royalty, and the very wealthy. They painted huge windows where there were none. They included columns, pillars and arches, adding richness, splendor and sophistication to the two-dimensional surfaces.

Years later the two were rivals in a painting contest. Each would try to create the more perfect illusion. Chuck was torn as to which painting to submit. He had painted the Connecticut River demonstrating the illusion of infinite extension by belaying the real bounds of its actual physical space. The river's vanishing point had been removed and space was projected infinitely. Foreground elements, such as grasses, rocks, and broken limbs were portrayed realistically.

Chuck chose to enter his rendition of a vineyard. The likeness of his plump, purple grapes hung in heavy bunches so natural looking that birds flew down to peck at them. Chuck was certain that in fooling the birds, he had easily won this contest.

Billy's offering to the competition entered partially draped with a cloth concealing the majority of the painting. Chuck unable to wait to see Billy's entry, reached out to lift the curtain. He was stunned to discover he had lost the contest. What had appeared to be a cloth curtain over his rival's painting was the illusion and he had been fooled.

Distraught at losing the painting competition, being fooled by Billy's painting, and feeling alone in the world, Chuck wandered around dazed. He stood in front of his Connecticut River painting and focused on the river's infinity and walked into the painting, absorbed into his own illusion, he was never seen again.

UNDYING LOVE

I T WAS WEDNESDAY, February 14, 1912 and the giggling Horton girls fixed each others hair, making clusters of ringlets. Their pink, silk brocade, dresses hung in a row ready for the 6:00 p.m. ceremony. Amelia, the fifth daughter, was the youngest of the eleven children and the last one to get married.

All five girls, accomplished seamstresses, had spent the past year pouring over Harpers Bazaar, and La Mode Pratique Magazines for ideas and pattern sheets, then sewed their own dresses. They out did themselves sewing elaborate, gowns with draped bustles, then heavily trimming them with pleats, flounces, frills and sashes. Amelia had hand sewn beads on her white satin, form-fitting, long-waisted, gown with a train.

With her hair pulled up, her slender silhouette looked more mature and sophisticated than her eighteen years.

Calvin and Amelia met when they were twelve years old. Calvin lived in Columbia, New Hampshire and Amelia lived on the other side of the Connecticut River in Lemington, Vermont.

The Columbia Covered Bridge spanned the river between New Hampshire and Vermont. It was a favorite spot of the locals both young and old.

It was still a mystery as to whom or what caused the fire in 1911 that destroyed the covered bridge. Amelia suspected Calvin knew more than he was saying. Calvin had proposed at the bridge on Valentine's Day last year, before the fire. It took nine months to rebuild the bridge.

The old Columbia Covered Bridge was Amelia's and Calvin's special place. It was where they met during the summer of 1906. It is where they read to each other, The Call of the Wild by Jack London. They sang, "In The Good Old Summertime," and "Take Me Out To The Ball Game." The old covered bridge is where they had first discussed Henry Ford's Model T, Orville and Wilbur Wright's flying machine and a huge passenger steam ship under constructed called the Titanic.

The old covered bridge between their two homes is where Calvin stole a peek at Amelia's diary, before he and Lester Miller had a fight over her in the eighth grade.

Years earlier as the Horton children started marrying and leaving home, their parents turned the seven bedroom homestead into a bed and breakfast. Lemington is thirty miles from Canada, two hundred miles from Boston, Massachusetts, two hundred sixty-five miles from Hartford, Connecticut and three hundred eighty miles from New York City.

The huge, romantic, home opened it's over sized, carved wood, front doors into a spacious hall featuring an attractive, wooden, winding staircase. There were two large parlors, each with its own stone fireplace on opposite sides of the main downstairs hall.

A variety of travelers from various social classes had made the bed and breakfast a well known, popular, colorful place. Travelers arrived by steamboat, train, on horseback and on foot. Scouts stopped for news. Trappers, in leather-fringed jackets paused on their way down the Connecticut River.

Local folks rented the parlors for parties, weddings, dances and gospel meetings. Most of the recent Horton brides had descended the winding staircase to meet their groom and guests. Today was the day Amelia would marry Calvin.

The aroma of cedar and pine logs, roses, lavender, sage, newly baked bread and venison roasting, greeted guests as they began to arrive. Candles burned in every window, all the guests were present and seated, but the bridegroom had not yet arrived.

The hour of the wedding came and the bridegroom still had not appeared. The anxious bride stood on an upstairs balcony watching for Calvin. Her veil, secured to chestnut brown ringlets, fluttered around her shoulders in the breeze. She refused to eat or to change out of her wedding gown. Standing and keeping watch in the moon light, Amelia's sisters wrapped her coat around her.

The guests ate the sumptuous supper then began to go home. Amelia's six brothers left to look for Calvin, then returned shortly with shocking news. His beaten body was found at the covered bridge.

Amelia finally gave way to despair and grief and the distraught young bride allowed her sisters to lead her to her bedroom. The next morning when they checked on her, she was gone. Some say they heard that she wandered out into the moonlight after Calvin, others claim she went into seclusion and died of a broken heart. There are those who think that Calvin's murderer, lay in wait and killed Amelia too or possibly she disappeared and took her own life.

The one consistent report over the years, is that on February 14th a beautiful, mysterious, young couple can been seen, dressed in vintage wedding clothing, wandering in Colebrook Village and out on U.S. Route 3 between Columbia, New Hampshire and Lemington, Vermont. They never speak and when approached, they disappear.

GREAT BIG BEAUTIFUL DOLL

CHARLOTTE WAS BORN in 1859, the youngest of seven children and the only girl with six older brothers. Her mother, Madaleine an only child born into a wealthy family married Charlotte's father when she was only sixteen years old. Maxwell Fuller was a successful entrepreneur and shrewd businessman in the textile industry and little Charlotte was the family's crown jewel.

Maxwell traveled the world purchasing, selling and lecturing. On one trip he brought Madaleine a loom and on another a new gadget, a lock stitch sewing machine.

As time went on, each of his six sons, Simon, Clayton, Gordon, Elton, Conrad and Nelson joined the business and developed and introduced new technology, organized labor, and imported/exported wool, cotton and silk. They established textile mills along the Connecticut River.

On a business trip to Germany, Maxwell brought back an unglazed porcelain Parian doll for Charlotte. It was identified by its hairstyle, called a covered wagon style (rather flat on top with sausage curls around the head). The doll's body was made of fine cotton stuffed with saw dust. It had hand carved wooden arms and legs. Charlotte immediately fell in love with her beautiful cerulean blue glass eyes.

Seeing the delight on the little girl's face, prompted her father to continue to look for dolls for Charlotte during his travels. Charlotte's brothers and their families started giving her dolls. Her father's associates sent gifts of dolls home for her and in a few short years, little Charlotte had an impressive, extensive, valuable, doll collection.

Her dolls were made of wax, china, wood, papier mache, bisque, leather, metal and clay. The collection contained baby dolls, character dolls, period dolls and high fashion dolls as well as French Bebes by Jumeau,Bru, Steinerand, Rohmer, Rorstead Royal Copenhagen and Jacob Petit. The dolls came from France, Germany, China, England, Poland,Czechoslovak, and Sweden.

Charlotte's favorite character dolls were Marie Antoinette, Dolley Madison, Mary Todd Lincoln and Alice In Wonderland.

Some dolls were rather crude while others had beautiful expressions with feathered brows and were exquisitely dressed. Charlotte loved them all the same. Her brothers, Simon and Gordon built a large shelving unit at the north end of her bedroom to display all of her dolls. She held and played with two special baby dolls but

Charlotte spent many hours in her room talking to and playing with her dolls. Feeling lazy, tired and weak she played on the floor. Her family didn't notice that she was getting sick and it came on so gradually that Charlotte herself didn't realize that she wasn't well. When a little tickle cough developed in her throat and chest she sucked on a cough drop after a cough drop until the symptoms disappeared.

One night when her father was on a business trip, her mother and three brothers still living at home were talking and laughing loudly, while playing board games at the dinning room table.

When the games were over, while putting things away they heard a weak, hacking cough coming from Charlotte's bedroom.

Madaleine went to the little girl's bedroom and discovered a weak and pale ten year old, feverish and unaware that she was coughing up blood.

The diagnosis was Tuberculosis. It had advanced quickly and gone untreated too long and Charlotte died. The family was devastated; they left Charlotte's room as it was and locked the door. Decades passed and the house and its furnishings remained in the family. Eventually the dolls were packed up, labeled, stored and forgotten in the attic. Generations later after no one in the family any longer wanted the house, it was sold. In dividing the family heirlooms in the attic, each descendent was invited to choose a doll from the outstanding, pristine, antique doll collection.

I had to be out of town that weekend and knowing they all were treasures, I asked my sister to choose one for me. Sunday night I got home late, exhausted. I dropped my keys, purse and over night bag at the hall table. I tossed my coat over the chair on my way to the bedroom. I caught a glimps of a great big beautiful life like looking doll sitting on the couch. My antique doll is larger than I remember any of them being when we unpacked them, I thought. I fell asleep as soon as my head hit the pillow.

The next morning I made coffee, unpacked my bag and started a load of laundry. I walked out on the sidewalk to get my newspaper when my sister drove up.

"I stopped by to drop off your doll on my way to work," she said, "and also, here is a little framed antique photo of Charlotte. I carried my newspaper, antique china doll and framed photo into the house. I was too stunned to tell my sister right then that I no longer live alone. My antique china doll rests on my book shelf beside the photo. But, my great big beautiful doll moves from spot to spot then sometimes disappears. I call her "Charlotte,"

THE LITTLE PEOPLE'S VILLAGE

W̶ITH BRYAN IT is always, let's make a deal. I'll go shopping if you'll go to the woodworking show, or if you go to the home improvement demonstration, then I'll go to the chick flick. That is why when I wanted to see a play at the Opera House, I was prepared to deal. I thought maybe he would offer a hockey game or window shopping for a truck. I was taken back when he said, I'll go if you'll go find the little people's village with me."

What? I had heard stories all my life, from my parents about a tiny stone village that was haunted. They had said that it was somewhere in Middlebury, Connecticut and that in the 1930's some lady spoke with and saw pixie-like creatures in the woods. She convinced her husband to build fourteen doll house size structures and a stone throne for her.

She refereed to herself as "The Queen Of The Little People." She either killed him and then herself or he killed her and then himself. If I had known the negotiation would involve hiking through a haunted woods in search of little people, I would have upped the anti, so I did.

"I'll go to Middlebury in search of little people in the haunted woods, if you go to the play at the Goodspeed Opera House in East Haddam on the Connecticut River. But wait, there's more, before the show we take the Lady Katherine dinner cruise. I've heard that the opera house is haunted too," I threw in to add to the appeal. A deal was struck.

The beautiful boat accommodated 200 people on the scenic two- hour cruise along the Connecticut River during the 5:30 buffet dinner. We were dropped off in plenty of time for the performance.

Bryan enjoyed the dinner cruise and play as much as I did so I thought maybe he would forget about the little people hunt. But, Saturday morning after we went out for breakfast as usual, we headed out Route 63 to the junction of 184. about a tenth of a mile on the right we parked and walked down the access road.

We squeezed past a huge prickly bush and there on the left side was the cutest abandoned little village. I was so mesmerized by the sight of the site that for a moment I had quit listening for pixie voices, or looking for ghosts and miniature people. There were fourteen very complex and detailed small stone houses. No two were alike. Some were A-framed and others were more traditional. All of them were three to four feet tall. I saw the normal size stone house where the man and his wife must have lived.

I was just beginning to come out of my sense of awe and once again start looking over my shoulder, and wincing at cracking sticks under foot. Yes, I even gasped when I saw what turned out to be a chipmunk.

I saw the throne I'd heard about, which was built in the side of the rock. For a moment I let my guard down and walked toward it.

"Are you the cops?" a male voice asked.

I froze in mid-step and probably with my mouth open. Bryan keep his composure and spoke with the two boys as they stepped out from hiding inside the larger ,stone house. They we're curious, just as we were and looking around.

They said they had been there before. The last time they took a lot of photographs and every photo had a white cloud printed in it that wasn't seen at the time. Taking photos is what brought them back, as did something they wanted to try.

I think they were embarrassed to tell us that they heard by chanting "Come out little people, come out little people," and some pixie, fairy-like creatures appeared.

Hoping no one was watching, we sat in a circle and chanted, "Come out little people, come out little people," but nothing happened. We held hands, concentrated ,focused and again chanted, "Come out little people, come out little people."

Still nothing happened. We felt foolish and laughed at ourselves.

The boys photographed the miniature houses, the large house and the throne, then the four of us walked back together. Back at the road they checked their cameras and there were no pictures.

PHOTOGRAPHER ACKNOWLEDGEMENTS

Cover Photograph of The Rocky Hill/Glastonbury Connecticut
Ferry Landing by N. Jason Godbey IV

Author's Photograph by Gerri Karamesinis
Karamesinis Photography, Vernon Connecticut

Photograph of The Goodspeed Opera House
East Haddam, Connecticut
by Mark G. Cappitella
http://www.MarksPhotographs.com